This wasn't a
convince him

This was...well, this was just letting a friend crash on the sofa, that was what it was. Carrying two bottles of beer, he rounded the corner from the kitchen and the full force of Sam's presence hit him.

At that moment Samantha Baldwin was everything he'd ever wanted, or would ever want in a woman, *want* being the operative word.

Sam's chest rose and fell gently, and Josh realised he'd been staring at her—staring at her chest, actually—for more than a few minutes. There was only so much chest-staring a woman would allow—and Josh knew from personal experience that it wasn't very much—before she objected. He swallowed. Sam wasn't objecting. Why wasn't she? She should object, dammit!

Josh met Sam's eyes, which were regarding him above a mouth curved in a Mona Lisa smile. Her hands slowly smoothed their way down her thighs, drawing his gaze. She was wearing a black skirt that outlined her legs as though they were immortalised in bronze.

She looked like a World War II pin-up photo.

She looked good. *Too good.*

And suddenly Josh knew he was going to be very, very bad...

Dear Reader,

The skirt is back! When you last saw the mysterious 'man-magnet' skirt, it was flying through the air at the end of Kristin Gabriel's *Seduced in Seattle*. However, Kristin, Cara Summers and I had so much fun writing this series, we decided someone should catch the skirt. And we also decided to give the next set of SINGLE IN THE CITY stories a twist…

For this instalment, we decided to have all three stories happen at the same time! Not only that, but the heroines are three relative strangers who end up becoming roommates in a New York apartment. Best of all, the books feature three lookalike skirts. But that's not all… You'll meet the neighbours—Mrs Higgenbotham and her poodle, Cleo, who is in therapy for Canine Intimacy Dysfunction, Petra, the sculptress with a penchant for naked men, and Franco, the aspiring actor/doorman with a gossip addiction. And of course, we'll introduce you to three new heroes, who may or may not have been attracted by the skirt.

With three women counting on the skirt to work its magic, mix-ups are bound to happen. Will they ever really be sure which skirt is which? Be sure to watch out for even more romantic misadventures next month in *Sheerly Irresistible* by Kristin Gabriel, then again in *Short, Sweet and Sexy*, by Cara Summers in August.

And be sure to visit our website at www.SingleintheCity.org to let us know how you like the series. While you're at it, check out my website at www.HeatherMacAllister.com for other writing news.

Happy reading!

Heather MacAllister

SKIRTING THE ISSUE

by

Heather MacAllister

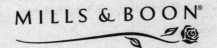
MILLS & BOON®

In memory of my grandmother,
Mildred Copple Hull.
1902–2002

*First published in Great Britain 2003
by Harlequin Mills & Boon Limited,
Eton House, 18-24 Paradise Road, Richmond, Surrey TW9 1SR*

© Heather W. MacAllister 2002

ISBN 0 263 83560 X

21-0603

*Printed and bound in Spain
by Litografia Rosés S.A., Barcelona*

Prologue

THERE WAS NOTHING LIKE A wedding to make a single woman assess her options. And Samantha Baldwin had options. She was hiding from one of them now.

"Sam! There you are."

She cringed. How had Kevin found her?

"The bride's about to throw the bouquet."

"Thanks for the warning." Caught behind the proverbial potted palm artfully disguising the hallway to the women's rest room, Sam downed the last swallow of her champagne and snagged another glass from a passing waiter.

"Won't it be difficult to catch the bouquet with your hands full?" Kevin, her boyfriend, her blond-haired, blue-eyed, what-a-wonderful-catch boyfriend, the very boyfriend who traveled to the wedding with her all the way from San Francisco to Seattle—even though she had told him not to—smiled archly. Sam didn't even know he knew how to smile archly. Kevin wasn't an arch sort of man. He was a veterinarian.

"Silly me." Looking him right in the eye, Sam quaffed the glass and handed it to him. "Oh, please," she said at his raised eyebrow. "The glasses are small and only half-full."

"I just want you to be sharp and alert."

It was a cue. She knew she was supposed to ask him

why she should be sharp and alert. Then he'd reply that it was so she could be sure and catch the bouquet. Then she'd ask why catching flowers was so important, and he'd...he'd...

And there the screen in Sam's mind went blank.

Or rather, she knew what was on the screen, she just wished she was in a different theater.

There were two shows running in Sam's mind. Showing on the screen with Kevin was the happily-ever-after, white-picket-fence, puppies-and-kids movie. A qualified thumbs-up, especially surrounded as she was by all the wedding vibes this weekend.

But showing on another screen was the promotion-and-corporate-success-in-New-York movie. Two thumbs-up. And in the audience, applauding wildly, was Sam's mother.

Kevin took her arm—really, there was no need; the glasses were small, a couple of swallows max—and gently, but insistently steered her toward the ballroom.

Sam swallowed dryly, since Kevin avoided the wait staff.

"Holy cow!" Kevin was given to animal imprecations. "Look at that mob."

"They can't all be wedding guests." But there they were all crowding around Kate and her bridesmaids, Chelsea, Gwen and Torrie. Sam felt cheered. The odds of her not catching the bouquet had just gone up.

At the realization, she looked up at Kevin guiltily, then back at Kate.

The other bridesmaids, all friends of Sam's from college, were also newlyweds and they all glowed disgustingly. No, it wasn't disgusting, but they were all so *happy* it made her wish for that happiness, too. The way they looked at their husbands—and the way their husbands looked back at them...Sam squeezed Kevin's arm and he looked down at her in almost the same way. He was a good man, a kind man—he cured little kids' sick puppies, for heaven's sake. But he also had a quirky sense of humor, played a ruthlessly wicked game of poker and was perfectly willing to walk out of a movie he didn't feel was worth his time.

She should love him. What was wrong with her that she didn't love him?

But she didn't. At least not enough to give up the chance of the promotion she was recently offered. And not enough to ask him to wait while she went to New York to compete for it. Because...because what if she got it? What if she became the east coast convention sales manager for Carrington Hotels? She'd have to move to New York. Kevin had a thriving veterinary practice in San Francisco. He'd have to really, really love her to relocate to New York.

And he'd deserve someone who really, really loved him back.

Sam squeezed his arm again and as he smiled down at her, she waited for the gooey feelings she knew Kate and the others felt for their husbands. She felt... fondness. And a little irritation because she didn't feel more.

That was it, then. She'd made her decision, the one she'd come all the way from San Francisco to think about. She'd intended to come alone, but Kevin had surprised her. Would it have made any difference if he'd stayed behind as she'd asked? She'd half-seriously quoted, "absence makes the heart grow fonder" at him, but he'd countered with, "while the cat's away, the mouse will play." The animal theme again, but honestly, she'd set herself up for it.

And speaking of setups...while Sam was pondering her future, Kevin steered her through an incredibly aggressive throng of single women until she'd reached a decent field position, one well within bouquet-throwing range. Then he'd kissed her on her cheek and got the heck out of Dodge.

Sam watched Kate search the crowd, her face lighting with radiant bliss—truly, she looked like the women in those diamond ads—when she found her husband. At her nod, Brock approached the bandleader, and then came a remarkable announcement: the bride would be throwing a skirt, not a bouquet.

Well, now. Sam edged toward the side. This she had to see. Oh, sure, she'd heard the rumors about this great skirt. Kate and her bridesmaids all swore they met their husbands while wearing it. Others must have heard about it, too, because as the bride and her attendants climbed the circular dais, they were practically mobbed.

Kate stepped forward and scanned the crowd. Taking a deep breath, she tossed the skirt high into the air, right toward the spot where Sam had been standing.

Then it seemed to float in the air, drifting left, as though caught by a draft from the ventilation system. It twirled and fluttered. It may have even glinted.

Then it dived. Straight toward Sam. Like she had a homing beacon attached to her, or something. Whatever, Sam ducked and waved her arms to fend off the attack. The crowd pushed and shoved, grasping for the black fabric. Sam backed up, and felt one of the white folding chairs against her calf. She lost her balance and grabbed blindly, hoping to prevent her fall. She grabbed a fistful of air—and the skirt. Astonishingly, the thing nearly molded itself to her hands, but it didn't prevent Sam from a hard landing on the dance floor. She sat, dazed, her legs splayed in front of her, the skirt in her hands.

The single women of Seattle gave a disappointed groan. Make that a menacing groan.

"Sam... You caught it! Way to go!" Kevin made his way through the knot of resentful women.

"But I didn't mean to catch it," Sam said. But she knew nobody heard her and wouldn't believe her if they had.

Kevin stood behind her and struggled to haul her upright by taking hold of her beneath her arms, almost like he was wrestling with a ninety-pound German shepherd.

Sam didn't weigh ninety pounds, but she was no German shepherd, either. She waved him off with skirt-covered hands and got to her feet.

"So, what's this mean?" he asked.

"That Kate wanted to dry her bouquet and keep it for herself?"

At that moment, Gwen, one of the bridesmaids, made her way toward them. "Hey, Sam!" She hugged her. "We were hoping you'd be the one." And Gwen smiled pointedly, beamed, actually, at Kevin.

Kevin was beaming back in perfect understanding. This was not good.

Gwen tapped the skirt with the pink rose she'd carried in the wedding. "Kate sent me over here to make sure you knew the skirt rules."

Sam held the skirt out in front of her. It shimmered enticingly. "There're rules?"

"Oh, yeah. Rules and a warning. It works fast."

"Is that the rule or the warning?"

Gwen laughed. "I got the skirt right after Christmas and I was married on Valentine's Day."

Sam stared at her. How horrible. Fortunately, she didn't say so.

"What exactly does it do?" Kevin asked.

"It attracts men," Gwen answered.

Kevin frowned.

"One of whom will be your true love," she added to Sam.

"What if she's already met her true love?" Kevin stepped forward and fingered the material of the skirt. It must have been a trick of the light, but the lustrous black material seemed to take on an ashy hue. It hung limply from Sam's hand.

"Then she'll know he's the one." Gwen gave one of the gooey smiles so prevalent today as a well-built man ambled over and tucked his arm around her waist. "After all, I already knew Alec, here, but it wasn't until I put on the skirt that I knew he was the one for me."

"If I recall, there was a certain red sweater you wore with it." Alec grinned. "I liked that sweater."

Gwen batted at his arm. "Anyway, when you find him, you'll know. And then you toss it at your wedding to some extremely lucky woman." After exchanging goo-goo eyes with her husband, Gwen went off with Alec.

Sam stared at the skirt and then at Kevin. He stared back. She knew all right, and she didn't need the skirt to tell her.

1

SUMMER IN NEW YORK CITY. It was...great. Really great to be here, Sam reminded herself. Just great. It would be greater if she could find an apartment, though. And she'd thought San Francisco rental prices were high.

But today, she was committed to making something happen. Nothing and nobody was getting to her today.

Dropping off a report with the receptionist, Sam headed for the banks of elevators that would take her from the executive offices to the fabulous lobby of Carrington's flagship hotel in Manhattan.

She rounded the corner in time to see an elevator close behind a tall man—being tall herself, Sam always noticed tall men. He was walking away from her with a confident loose-limbed stride that seemed vaguely familiar. He wore a sports coat that she could see was well-cut, though the plaid was too loud for her taste, just like the jackets Josh—

She froze, staring at the back of the man's head. No. This man didn't remind her of anyone, certainly not anyone who might jinx the day for her.

Certainly not Josh Crandall, scourge of the convention sales circuit and Sam's own personal nemesis.

An involuntary shudder rippled through her. Nope. Not Josh Crandall. Couldn't be. Sam got into the express elevator and rode it all the way to the lobby. She had left Josh Crandall far, far behind. *He* was still scrambling—in his usual underhanded, sneaky way— to book conventions for Meckler Hotels, while she, who prided herself on honesty and fair dealings, was about to become Carrington's east coast sales manager.

Sam exited the hotel and crossed Forty-second Street on her way to the post office. She was currently staying in a substandard room at the Manhattan Carrington. Once maintenance repaired the problem—the air-conditioning wasn't as enthusiastic as it needed to be— then she would move to another unrentable room. She'd been living like this for two weeks now and this weekend, her housing vouchers, such as they were, ran out. Sure, she could have an employee discount, but even with that, the hotel was too pricey to stay in the whole summer.

Today, Sam had been at her desk two hours early and was taking a long lunch, determined to find some place to live, or at least a cheaper hotel.

She pushed open the door to the post office, thankful for the air-conditioning. She did miss San Francisco's temperate weather.

Because it was noontime, there was a line at the post office, but Sam figured there was always going to be a line in New York and she might as well get used to it. Sam got at the end of the line, which looped back on itself three times like an amusement park ride. Since all the clerk windows were open, the wait shouldn't be more than twenty minutes or so. And if it was longer, well, what could she do about it?

She fanned herself with her soft bulky package. In it was the skirt. She'd never had so much attention as she'd had since catching the thing at Kate's wedding. School friends she hadn't heard from in years had contacted her for progress reports. And magazines, too, for pity's sake! There had been articles about the thing. And not one, but *two* reporters had tracked her down here in New York.

And then there were all the women who'd e-mailed her to check on her progress. Good grief. She hadn't even worn the thing, not counting that hideous evening right after she'd caught it when Kevin had insisted that she try it on and she'd hoped it wouldn't fit.

It had. It had fit as though it had been made for her. Sam was a tall woman—five-ten in flats which she wore because she felt like it and not to de-emphasize her height—and the skirt flirted with the top of her knees.

Kevin had wanted to flirt with the top of her knees, too, and insisted she wear the new addition to her wardrobe to dinner. *He* loved the skirt. Sam couldn't see why. It was black and maybe shorter than she generally wore, but not outrageously so. Nothing special. The material that had seemed so rich and warmly luxurious earlier was now sleazy and limp. It wasn't doing anything for her. Unfortunately, neither was Kevin. She didn't want to wear it to dinner, which Kevin had taken as an invitation to skip dinner for other pursuits when that hadn't been Sam's intention *at all.*

Kevin had become obnoxious and Kevin was never obnoxious. He'd made a cryptic remark about willing to buy the whole cow instead of settling for milk—another animal metaphor—and that she should appreciate it. She didn't. They'd argued and Sam had been forced to tell him right then that she'd decided to come to New York after all.

He'd blamed the skirt, which was so incredibly stupid she couldn't believe it, but, understanding that his pride had been hurt, Sam had allowed it.

She never intended to wear the skirt again, let alone throw it at her nonexistent wedding. Why would she want to mess up her life just when it was getting interesting? And the thing that really chapped her was that Kevin had just *assumed* that Sam would give up her chance at a promotion to stay in San Francisco with him. It never occurred to him to move to New York with her, not that she wanted him to, but still. He never *got* it; he never understood that he expected *her* to make the big sacrifice without considering making one of his own.

The sound of crumpling paper as she squeezed the package brought Sam back to the present.

Inhaling, she cleared her mind of all things Kevin. New York air could do that to a person. In spite of her mother's tempting suggestion that she do all womankind a favor and burn it, Sam intended to mail the skirt back to Kate. That's all there was to it.

She smoothed out the label. Let Kate invite some desperately single candidates to an elegant little luncheon where she could use all her bridal china and throw the thing at them.

Exhaling, Sam massaged the muscles in her neck, relaxing because for once, no one she knew was watching her or comparing her to the other job candidates.

Yes, competing for a position was a particularly ef-

fective form of torture in hotel management circles, no
doubt thought of by a high-paid consultant who'd
never actually experienced the unrelenting pressure of
being scrutinized for days on end. Carrington's executive board was always hiring consultants. If she got the
job—and maybe if she didn't—she was going to tell
them what they could do with their consultants. Dip-
lomatically, of course, because even though somebody
was going to crack soon, it wasn't going to be Sam.

There were to have been four candidates for the position of east coast convention sales manager, but one
had declined, citing a reluctance to relocate to New
York City—the wimp—so it was now Sam and two
men. Her mother had been calling for nightly updates
and to give Sam feminist pep talks. Sam's mother had
been a foot soldier in the war between the sexes and
considered Sam one of her best weapons.

Sam was perfectly willing to be a weapon. As the
youngest of four girls, she hadn't often had her
mother's undivided attention—if ever—and enjoyed
talking strategy and letting off steam.

This past week, managers from all the hotels in the
eastern quadrant of the United States had been meeting at the flagship Carrington near Times Square. Sam
and her two colleagues had been running meetings,
preparing theater outings, and getting to know the
managers and their hotels. Of course Sam had met
some of them before when she'd contracted with
groups to hold conventions at their hotels, but as the
east coast manager, she'd be expected to become familiar with all the little quirks about their hotels. It
wouldn't hurt to get chummy with them, either, her

mother reminded her, but Sam wasn't a chummy sort of person. Some people just didn't know the difference between chummy and suggestive. Josh Crandall, for instance.

Or they did and ignored it.

Like Josh Crandall.

The line moved forward and Sam hunched her shoulders, wishing she'd splurged on a massage with the hotel masseuse. Today was judgment day. There was only one meeting—one big, giant, important, possibly life-altering meeting—and Sam and the other candidates weren't attending. Their convention sales records were being scrutinized. Sam had a spectacular sales record—except for two blotches. Sizable blotches, if she were being truthful. And both were courtesy of Josh Crandall of Meckler Hotels.

Sam closed her eyes. The very thought of him made her stomach queasy, the kind of queasy she got after eating too much chocolate in a short amount of time, which she usually did after going head-to-head with Josh.

Recently he'd been turning up every time she had a presentation. And now she was imagining him. She opened her eyes and checked out the people in line with her, involuntarily looking for his dark, carefully tousled hair and deceptively casual, but well-cut plaid sports coat. Oh, and the smile. That you-want-me-and-we-both-know-it smile.

She hated that smile. And he knew it.

Sam had a sudden craving for M&M's.

Even now, the Carrington brass were probably dissecting her failed proposals. They'd been perfect, she knew, but still each convention had chosen Josh and the Meckler chain over Carrington. And because her proposals had been perfect, that meant the decisions had been based on intangibles, such as the charm of the representatives. In other words, they'd liked Josh better than Sam, which meant the failure had been hers, personally. Josh had no problem being chummy. Or suggestive, either.

It wasn't that she'd never bested him before—or after—those incidences, it was that since then, she'd been too quick to make concessions to Carrington's profit margin in order to ensure she never lost to him again.

The last time...Sam sucked her breath between her teeth—she *really* needed some chocolate—the last time, she'd cut profit to the bone. But instead of countering, Josh had laughed—his laughs dripped with evil amusement—then admitted he hadn't wanted the convention anyway because the group in question was known for damaging hotel rooms.

And they had. Sam winced.

So, maybe Josh had won *three* times.

Stop thinking about him. It would only make her crazy. Sam deliberately wiped Josh and his smile from her mind and concentrated on the people around her. There were a couple of conversations going on—office workers mailing company letters and two good-looking, well-dressed men, well-dressed if she discounted the leather cowboy vest one wore and she was inclined to until she realized it was fake leather. And...and that the green color was *not* a trick of the light. Still, even with green faux leather with, she swallowed, silver fringe, they compared favorably to Josh and his stupid plaid jackets—if she'd been thinking about Josh, which she wasn't.

The two men were one loop behind Sam and approached her as the line wound toward the counter windows. One man held a stack of printed postcards and the other man stuck preaddressed labels on them.

"Tavish, every year you go through this," said the man with titanium glasses. "Stop waiting until the last minute."

"But I always find a sublet," replied Tavish, the taller of the two.

Sam liked tall men and it had nothing to do with her own height. Josh was tall—not that it mattered.

"But you don't even investigate the tenants first!"

Tavish stuck on another label. "I go by instinct."

"Someday your instincts are going to leave you with a trashed apartment."

"Then it'll be time to redecorate." He looked off into the distance. "I'm growing weary of sage."

If he'd asked, Sam could have told him what colors were predicted to be popular in the next couple of years. Carrington was building a new hotel in Trenton and she'd seen the reports from the decorating team. Colors were going to be clean and complex, whatever that meant. She made a mental note to find out. It might be important for her to know.

"And you always send these cards. Haven't you heard of e-mail?"

"Who can keep up with everyone's e-mail address? All those letters and dots and symbols..." Tavish grimaced.

"Who can keep up with your summer addresses?"

"That's why I send the cards."

The men had moved behind her. Sam was now passing by the supply counter and people kept reaching in front of her for forms, labels and envelopes. She was relieved when she moved by it, looped around, and several minutes later faced the two men again. Tavish was still peeling off labels and sticking them on his postcards. He apparently had a large acquaintanceship.

"Didn't you just go on safari a couple of years ago?"

Tavish laughed, a warm rich chuckle that was oh-so-different from Josh's predatory cackle—not that she was thinking about Josh Crandall while standing in line at a New York City post office. That would be foolish.

"There are safaris and there are safaris," Tavish replied.

"An elephant is an elephant is an elephant."

"But the aptly named Mona Virtue will be a member of the group."

"Ah." They both laughed.

Men.

"Some men have all the luck."

"I make my own luck." Tavish held out his hand for another postcard.

The other man nodded. "I'll have to admit that holding a lottery for a Central Park West apartment is genius."

"Thank you."

Sam had been idly eavesdropping but hearing about the apartment again made her focus her attention even though Central Park West was so out of her league.

"And you don't even advertise."

"I don't have to."

The movement of the line brought the men closer to Sam and the supply table. People kept cutting through the line which interfered with her eavesdropping.

"...agents do screen, so I'm not taking the wild risk you seem to think."

"Risk, or not, didn't you tell everyone to be there at noon?"

Both men checked their watches. Sam did as well. It was twelve-thirty.

Tavish shrugged. "They'll wait." He spoke with supreme confidence.

His apartment was being shown at noon. His unadvertised apartment. A sublet. Knowing what she did of New York, Sam knew the sublet was likely illegal. The fact that this didn't bother her must mean something, but Sam wasn't going to explore that now. This man in the fake leather cowboy vest had an apartment for rent. Sam needed an apartment. There was no need to complicate matters.

Except maybe to wonder in what kind of apartment a man who wore a fake leather cowboy vest in June might live, but wasn't that what posters, pillows and artfully placed colorful throws were for?

As the men approached, Sam strained to see the return address on the postcards Tavish labeled. NY, NY. Yeah, yeah. Tell her something she didn't know: She leaned closer, but at that moment, someone trying to cut through the line jabbed her with an elbow, then bumped into Tavish and his friend.

"Hey, watch it, buddy." Mr. Titanium Glasses made

a rude gesture as several of the postcards fell to the grimy floor.

Not proud, Sam grabbed for one. She intended to give it back—truly she did—but somehow, in the commotion, a strong self-preservation instinct kicked in. She read the printing, "Tavish McLain announces his summer itinerary. In June, he will be on safari and can be reached in care of Mavis Trent Travel..." In July, he'd be summering at a villa in Italy. And so on until Labor Day. Sounded like a great summer. Better than hers, even if she did get the promotion. Must be nice. Sam flipped the card over and there, printed in the upper left-hand corner, was an address.

It had to be his apartment. It had to be.

I make my own luck. Well then. If this wasn't a sign, she didn't know what was.

Without giving herself time to reconsider, Sam kept the card and walked out of the post office, hailed a cab, then gave them the address of the apartment.

The man ran a lottery for his apartment. She couldn't win if she didn't play the game.

AFTER FLINGING WAY TOO much money—guilt, no doubt—at the cabbie, Sam climbed out of the taxi and looked quickly up and down the street.

Nice neighborhood.

Who was she kidding? *Fabulous* neighborhood. The kind where all the apartment buildings had snooty uniformed doormen. Except this one, it seemed. There was no doorman, uniformed or otherwise.

Maybe he was performing one of those errands everyone seemed to have doormen perform. Sam only knew this from movies and television and not from personal experience. But she could learn. Would love to learn, in fact.

She pushed open the plate-glass door. And shouldn't that be a duty of a *door*man? she was thinking when her eyes were assaulted by a tableau featuring a man with a pale, hairless chest smack dab in the tiny foyer.

Actually, he was smack dab on a folding lawn chair as he soaked his feet in a plastic wading pool featuring cartoon fishes. He wore baggy blue polka-dot swimming trunks, which clashed with the blue wading pool, she noted, as well as with the lime-green zinc oxide he painted on his nose. And...could that possibly be the Beach Boys? Yes. Definitely the Beach Boys.

"Password?" he shouted over "Surfin' U.S.A." He slid his mirrored sunglasses down his nose, which got them gunked up with the zinc oxide.

Password? She should have known good luck always came with a catch. Sam wondered if the password bore any resemblance to the name of a dead president and wished she hadn't been so generous to the cab driver.

While she considered her next move, the man cleaned the green stuff off his sunglasses and reapplied more to his nose. "I'm waaaaiiiiting," he sang. Then he cleared his throat and sang it again an octave lower, adding a theatrical vibrato. "Not bad. Certainly good enough for off Broadway, not that there are many musicals off Broadway these days. But better than the dinner theater circuit, wouldn't you say?"

"I wouldn't presume to say anything."

"I noticed." He slipped the glasses back into place. "Don't know the password? How about a piece of juicy gossip?"

"I've only got this." Sam held up the card she'd filched at the post office.

"So you *are* here about the apartment. You're late."

"I know, but Tavish didn't say anything about a password."

"Consistency." He gestured outward, as though reciting Shakespeare. "All I ask is consistency. Is that too much to ask?"

Sam did a little gesturing of her own toward the beach setup. "I think you ask a lot more than that."

He stared at her—or maybe not. With the mirrored sunglasses covering his eyes, she couldn't tell. "I like you. You may pass." He waved her toward the elevator.

"Thanks, uh..."

"Franco Rossi, at your service." He assumed the manner of a Spanish grandee, rolling his hand and inclining his head.

"Thanks, Franco."

"Do run along. You're blocking the light."

Oooookay. Sam didn't need to be told twice. Jabbing the button on the elevator, she stared at the numbers above the door and willed the car to come.

The Beach Boys swelled for a brief moment then retreated.

"Who are you?" Sam heard.

The elevator arrived and she nearly pulled open the doors herself. Escaping inside, she turned and saw a woman talking to the weird doorman, or whatever he was, and another pulling open the heavy plate-glass door.

"Password?" she heard just before the doors closed.

Great. More competition. She hoped there weren't any more rules she didn't know about.

2

THE APARTMENT WAS ON THE sixth floor. Just enough to get a modest workout, if Sam were so inclined. There were only three apartments on the floor and number 6C was at the end. Sam didn't even have to look at the card. She could hear the crowd the moment she stepped off the elevator.

What was she doing here? This was hopeless.

But Sam had been in hopeless situations before—generally those including Josh Crandall...*why* couldn't she stop thinking about him? Anyway, some of those had turned out to be not so hopeless after all because she'd persevered and that's what she planned to do now. She'd persevere herself right into the apartment.

Sam opened the door. Why knock? No one would hear her.

The first thing she noticed was that the ratio of women to men was about, well, except for a couple of men who appeared to be brokers, the ratio was ninety-eight to two. The next thing she noticed was that there was a high percentage of blondes in the mix, including a woman with pink-blond hair and matching poodle.

Sam was very definitely not a blonde.

People were freely milling around, so Sam acted like she belonged there and milled as well. The apartment appeared to have three bedrooms, though one was currently being used as a combination office and video lair.

Definitely bachelor pad material. She looked upward, expecting mirrors, but apparently Tavish's excruciating taste extended only to cowboy vests. Maybe a touch of overkill on the Western look—how many steer horns did a person need?—but, hey, this was great. Fabulous location, near the Metropolitan Museum of Art, generously spaced for a New York apartment, and she could always rent out the other bedrooms to help with the rent.

Would that be a sub-sublet? Was that more illegal than a regular sublet?

"Where is Tavish?" pouted one blonde.

One of the men stood on the staircase leading to a small loft. "Mr. McLain will be here momentarily."

"I say we can start without him," said another blonde. This one wore a black suit and nearly black lipstick, spike heels and had her hair in a French twist that not one strand dared to come loose.

Sam tucked her own windblown hair—that would be brown windblown hair—behind her ears and straightened her spine.

"My opening offer will be fifteen hundred," the woman continued. She looked over the competition. "So anyone who can't beat that is out of luck because the price *will* go higher."

"But...but I don't understand!" It was a redhead. The only one. "Tavish promised me the apartment for eight-fifty!"

"He promised *me* I could have it for eight hundred!" said someone else.

"Oh, honey." The blond woman who'd taken charge shook her head. "He does this every year. Then a few of us spend the following year bribing him in hopes he'll just forget this demeaning lottery and let one of us have the apartment for the summer." She looked wistful. "I actually lived here one summer. It was..." She seemed to remember where she was and that a crowd of apartment competitors hung raptly on each word. "Just be prepared to ante up, kiddos."

Sam had been mentally plundering her savings as the door opened and the two women she'd seen in the lobby entered the apartment. They must have known the password.

One of them, poor thing, actually was dragging luggage with her. She looked desperate. Desperate enough to bid a lot. Sam swept an assessing gaze over her. She didn't look as though she had a lot to bid.

The woman next to her was an unknown. A blond unknown, though. Unsmiling, she looked like a woman with a mission—and Sam knew what the mission was. Sam watched her case the situation from the edge of the crowd, bracing herself for when they locked eyes.

Actually, it wasn't much of a lock. Sam figured she didn't come across as much competition when the woman's gaze swept past her after the briefest hesitation. Probably because she wasn't a blonde.

French Twist held a check high over her head. "Here it is, folks. Good faith money. Forty-five hundred dollars—three months—up front." She walked over to one of the agents and tried to hand him a check.

"Hey!" someone shouted, and that pretty much set the rest of the potential renters off.

Some headed for the door and Sam got carried along with them. She didn't fight too much because she wasn't yet sure that staying would do any good. Just how much higher would she have to go? Though facing Central Park would be a kick, she didn't need three bedrooms and there would be the hassle of trying to find roommates for just the summer—even assuming she could outbid French Twist.

The exodus toward the door backed up as the first of the crowd got held up at the elevator. Sam stepped out of the current of disappointed women and found herself next to the two she'd seen downstairs. The one with the luggage was sitting on her suitcase staring blankly at the crowd. The other one, the short blonde, was studying her checkbook and had whipped out her cell phone.

Sam spoke to the woman on the suitcase. "This is really something, isn't it?"

"Not exactly what I expected," the woman answered, motioning to the suitcases. "I was planning to move in here today. Now, I don't know what I'm going to do."

Sam knew despair when she heard it. "This is your lucky day. I work for a hotel. Therefore, I can promise you won't sleep on the street tonight. And you can treat yourself to a nice, hot bubble bath."

"I can't—"

"Oh, I got that part. You'd be in one of the unrentable rooms. No charge."

Her eyes narrowed in suspicion. "Why would you do that? You don't even know me."

Oh, good grief. When had a good deed become a threat? "Because I can. Because helping the sisterhood was something my mother drilled into me. And, hey, I get off on warm, fuzzy feelings in my tummy."

There was a crack of laughter from the other woman. "So do I, but they don't come from giving away freebie hotel rooms," the woman said with a smile.

Sam grinned down at her. "Samantha Baldwin." She stuck her hand out at the exact moment the other woman stuck out hers.

"A. J. Potter. You sounded like a madam gathering the poor waif into her house of ill repute. I already made the same great impression. I think we scared her."

"I'm not scared," denied the other woman, still sitting on her suitcase. "Just fascinated by abnormal human behavior. Abnormal for a New Yorker, anyway."

A.J. turned her attention back to Sam. "This place has three bedrooms."

Ooo. She cut right to the chase. Sam liked her. "I don't smoke. I can go eighteen hundred a month, but I don't want to."

"Non-smoker, I'm in for two grand."

"You'd get the big bedroom, then."

They looked down. "What's your name?" A.J. asked the woman on the suitcase.

"Claire Dellafield. Why?"

Sam gestured to her. "Get with the program. We're forming a rental coalition. You want in?"

Claire stood, revealing that she was as short as A.J. "You mean we'd room together?"

"Mental functions appear to be intact," A.J. said. "You smoke?"

Claire shook her head. "But I can learn."

Sam laughed. "She's in for the entertainment value alone."

"How much can you contribute to rent?" A.J. was displaying a practical side.

Claire drew a deep breath. "Eight hundred."

"That's forty-six hundred." A.J. exhaled. "Surely the rent won't go as high as that."

They looked at the remaining women arguing with the brokers.

"Then again," Sam began, just as the door opened and the men from the post office walked into the room.

"Tavish!" several voices squealed. Others snarled.

"Let this play out," A.J. advised and Sam totally agreed.

The three of them watched women practically pawing at Tavish. Sam hoped one of them would paw off his green vest, but no such luck.

The more she watched, the more her hopes sank. Sam had spent years honing her negotiating skills and knew that the key to a successful deal was figuring out what the other guy really wanted and seeing that he got it. Tavish, she realized, wanted to be adored by his social circle—or the social circle he wanted to, uh, circle in. She remembered French Twist talking about bribing him during the year and remembered his summer itinerary—he was "guesting" everywhere.

Clearly, the key to this deal was more than money.

Tavish would probably rent out his apartment even if he weren't going anywhere for the summer.

Sam glanced at her two potential roommates. She liked A.J. already. Claire, she didn't know as well, but she had potential. They needed an edge. Something to offer. Something to make them attractive renters to Tavish.

She was figuring out how much it would cost her to let Tavish throw a ritzy party in the flagship Carrington's presidential suite when she refocused on the scene. All those beautiful blond women vying for his attention...he was lapping it up.

Though A.J. did have blond hair, Sam couldn't see her as the fawning type.

Sam shifted her package to the other arm. The thing was so hot. She didn't need to feel hot right now. She needed to *be* hot...

Sam stared at the wrapping surrounding the skirt. Yeah, sure it was supposed to be a real man magnet, but that was just a story, right? It didn't really...

"Stand in front of me," she said to the other two, as she tore off the brown paper.

Claire's eyes widened as Sam unzipped her skirt. "What are you doing?"

Sam told them the gist of the skirt legend as she pulled it on.

"You're kidding." A.J. looked as though she wanted to reconsider rooming with Sam.

"Look, I don't believe it, either, but it can't hurt." She handed her jacket to Claire and smoothed the skirt over her thighs.

It *was* a great fit. Must be another sign. They were meant to have the apartment.

"Follow me, ladies." As Sam walked forward, the black fabric whispered over her legs and she found herself changing the way she walked in order to accommodate it.

She imagined herself walking in slow motion, hair rippling over her shoulders, her eyes on the prize—Tavish.

As she drew closer, the women moved to one side, eyeing her and the two behind her. Sam cut right through until she was standing directly in front of Tavish, the two brokers, and French Twist.

"Hello," she purred.

Three pairs of male eyes swiveled her way.

"I'm Samantha Baldwin." She held out her hand and Tavish stepped forward to grasp it.

"Tavish McLain." He took her hand and held it, never once blinking.

The two brokers attempted to introduce themselves, but Tavish wouldn't relinquish Samantha's hand.

Propelling Claire with her, A.J. stepped into the breach and occupied the brokers.

"You have the perfect apartment," Sam cooed. All this cooing and purring was new to her, but it was amazing what it did.

"I c-call it home," Tavish stuttered, still holding Sam's hand.

"I'd like to call it home, too—for the summer at least." She sent him a limpid gaze and squeezed his hand.

"Well, I...well, I'm sure—"

"Just a minute! *I've* given you a check for forty-five hundred dollars!" French Twist wasn't giving up.

"Roger, give Meredith back her check," Tavish instructed.

"So I'll give you another for six thousand." Boy, the woman was persistent.

"Would you want all the rent up front?" Sam asked.

Tavish creased his brow. "Oh, no, no, no. Not if it wouldn't be convenient for you."

Sam still held Tavish's gaze. He still held her hand. She was going to have to blink soon or her eyes would start watering, but he seemed utterly entranced by her and she wanted to take advantage. What she really wanted to do was quickly scribble out a check.

Fortunately, A.J. had grasped the situation. Sam heard a rip and a blue rectangle appeared in Sam's peripheral vision. With her free hand she took the check and offered it to Tavish.

"Here you go...two thousand dollars." Two thousand? A.J. should have tried for fifteen hundred. Still two thousand a month split three ways was within all their budgets.

Tavish smiled. "So you want to pay all the rent up front, after all?"

All the rent? Sam's heart picked up speed.

Tavish stuck the check in his vest pocket. "The perfect tenant, wouldn't you say Roger?"

"I'd say so." One of the brokers inched closer.

"But wait, I thought that was just for—ow!" Claire broke off.

"That should be tenant*s*." Sam gestured behind her. "My roommates." She risked breaking eye contact to glance at them. A.J. waggled her fingers. Claire gave a tight smile and rubbed her arm.

"Gentlemen, which one of you has the papers we should sign?" A.J. tried to get the brokers' attention.

"Papers?" One spoke but he was looking at Sam.

A.J. snapped her fingers in front of his face. "An indemnity clause? Terms of lease? Liability release?"

That's right—get that laughably low rent in there before Tavish came to his senses.

"Uh, right here." The broker fumbled in his breast pocket.

Claire linked her arm around the other broker's. "You and I are on crowd control. Thanks for coming everybody!" she called and waved them toward the door.

"Hey!" French Twist wasn't budging.

"Ta-ta, Meredith. Just think, you won't have to walk Cleo."

"I would have hired a walker for that damn poodle, and you know it!"

"As you did last time. Mrs. Higginbotham said that Cleo was very stressed."

Poodle? Was dog sitting part of the deal? Sam blinked. She couldn't help it. Fortunately, breaking eye contact didn't seem to diminish her strange power over Tavish. "Do you have a dog?" she asked in a breathy voice.

Tavish shook his head.

Okay, then. Things were just hunky-dory. A.J. was handling the contract and Claire was making everybody leave.

Sam's hand was sweating. Or it could have been

Tavish's. Probably both. How was she supposed to extricate herself? She now not only believed, she thoroughly understood the "magnet" part of the skirt's legend. Except how did she turn it off?

"I CAN'T BELIEVE YOU DID IT!" A.J. gave her a high five, which Sam was glad she could high-five back, because she thought she'd *never* get her hand back from Tavish. Then Claire high-fived her. Then they high-fived each other—or low-fived, since they were both so much shorter than Sam.

Then Sam took off the skirt. They were alone after having made enemies of a significant percentage of the blondes in New York City, but Sam didn't care. She'd found an apartment—and for a ridiculously low rent. Don't ask her how that happened.

A.J., who'd turned out to be a lawyer—and how handy was that?—had put the amount right into the rental agreement.

"I've got to get back to the hotel," Sam called, hating to abandon her new roommates before getting to know them. She'd been really lucky there. The three of them appeared to be on the same wavelength, which was reassuring considering how many different wavelengths there were in New York City.

Carefully folding the skirt—she wasn't mailing it anywhere after today—Sam put it on the top shelf in the second largest bedroom and put her suit skirt back on. "Let's have dinner together here," she called.

"I'll get takeout," A.J. offered.

"Sounds fab. If I can, I'll see if the pastry chef has an extra Sacher torte and contribute that."

"What's Sacher torte?" Claire asked.

"Think dense chocolate. Sin on a fork." Sam grabbed her purse. "I hate to leave you guys like this, but I really need to get back to work."

"Like I'm going to complain after you rescued me," Claire said.

"Ditto." A.J. shooed her away. "Go."

And Sam went. She was on top of the world. She didn't know if it was fate, or the skirt, but Tavish had practically *given* them the apartment.

The other potential renters hadn't been pleased, to understate matters, but Sam didn't care. She'd taken a chance and look how it had paid off.

Today, she was invincible. Invulnerable. Triumphant. The promotion was as good as hers.

Humming—it *was* the Beach Boys, but who cared after the day she'd had—Sam strode into the lobby of the Carrington and punched the button for the executive offices. The doors parted immediately. It was just that kind of day.

Going to the top floor without stopping—she was on such a roll—the doors whisked open. Sam stepped into the foyer of the executive offices half expecting a general hush followed by a trumpet fanfare.

Look out world, Sam Baldwin has arrived. She strode, yes, strode, toward the skimpy temporary office she was using. She should really ask for something better. With her luck today, she'd probably get a corner office.

"Tiffany, any messages?" She'd always wanted to say that.

Tiffany, the receptionist, gave her an annoyed look,

completely failing to notice Sam's aura of power. "I don't know—check your voice mail. Oh, actually, you might go see Mr. Hennesey. He was looking for you right after lunch." Tiffany pointedly looked at her watch. "Like, about an hour ago."

"Too bad he wasn't looking for me at seven-thirty this morning when I was at my desk."

Tiffany was clearly going nowhere. She'd be singing a different tune once Sam was promoted.

Sam went in search of Mr. Hennesey. Odd. She would have thought he'd still be in the meeting. But no. She could hear him talking with someone in his office.

"Mr. Hennesey?" Sam knocked on the open door before stepping inside. "Tiffany said you were looking for me. If it's about the profit comparison for Happy Hours with and without complimentary buffets, I came in early this morning and finished the report. I left it with Tiffany."

"Great. I'll check with her in a bit." Mr. Hennesey leaned against the corner of his desk, clearly in no hurry.

So much for early-morning brownie points. Sam felt her aura dim just a bit.

"Actually, I was looking for you because I understand you're acquainted with our new sales consultant."

Sam's neck tickled as the hairs on the back stood up. It was her only warning that her roll had ended, splatting right into the figure she hadn't noticed sitting in Mr. Hennesey's leather love seat.

Her aura tarnished.

Her luck came up snake eyes.

Her good mood fizzled.

She slid off the top of the world.

Slowly, she turned her head, something within her already knowing the identity of the man, the one aura-tarnishing person she knew…

Josh Crandall.

He grinned—no, leered…no, it was a smirk. Definitely a smirk. "Hiya, Sam. How's tricks?"

How's tricks. Nobody said that anymore—nobody outside of Mr. Hennesey's generation. *Doing a little intergenerational bonding, Mr. Crandall?*

On the other hand, being tricky was Josh's modus operandi.

He didn't bother to stand because that would show respect and heaven forbid Josh Crandall should show respect for anyone he didn't have to.

Sam would rise above the situation, which meant she could lower herself and *still* be above him.

"Mr. Crandall." What was he doing here?

"Oh, take the ruler out of your—" He shifted and unrepentantly cleared his throat, his meaning crystal clear. "I told Bill, here, we were buds."

"Professional buds," Sam clarified, though Josh didn't have a professional bone in his body and she was no more his "bud" than…better not go there.

"If you insist." His grin widened and he winked.

Sam wished she had a really good set of fingernails so she could scratch that grin off his loathsome face. Even so, she could feel what fingernails she had digging into her palms. In a couple of short sentences, he'd completely changed Bill Hennesey's picture of her—

and not for the better. Too much was at stake for Sam to allow Josh to get away with it.

"I do insist, as you well know." She sent a deliberately casual smile toward Mr. Hennesey. "Josh and I have crossed paths on the convention circuit the past couple of years. He's very good at what he does." *But what he does isn't very good.*

She congratulated herself on her word choice. Outwardly, it was a compliment. Maybe Josh would reciprocate.

"Why, *thank* you, Sam. Glad to hear you didn't have any complaints."

Or maybe not.

Naturally, Mr. Hennesey chuckled. "Yes, he is, which is why we're delighted to hire his company to train our staff."

What company? "You mean Meckler?"

"Josh has left Meckler Hotels and has started his own sales training company."

Josh leaned forward and dangled a business card from his fingers. Sam had to walk over to him and reach over the tiny coffee table in order to take it.

If Mr. Hennesey weren't there, she would have ripped it into confetti and thrown it in Josh's face. But Mr. Hennesey *was* there, more's the pity, so Sam politely took the card, and looked at it. *Josh Crandall, Perfect Pitch Sales Seminars.*

Now what? With her back to Mr. Hennesey, Sam eyed Josh suspiciously. Was this another of his slick tricks? Devious ways? Underhanded maneuvers?

Josh gave her a blandly innocent smile which Sam didn't buy for an instant.

Mr. Hennesey apparently did. "Josh has been so successful in convention sales—" Sam winced, knowing at whose expense a few of those successes came, "—that I was eager to give him the opportunity to share some of his secrets."

"You're actually willing to go on record?" she said to Josh.

"For a price."

"Well, we always knew you had a price."

"Everybody's got a price, chickie, even you." He threw one of his casual smiles at Mr. Hennesey. "Finding a person's price is one of the strategies I'll cover in my seminar."

Slick, slimy and smooth. Vintage Josh. Sam gritted her teeth.

Mr. Hennesey was clearly mesmerized by him, but then most people were. Young, old, male, female. Everybody liked Josh. He made them feel good when they were with him which made them want to please him so he'd stick around. So they'd please him by giving Meckler Hotels their convention business. But then he'd leave anyway. Didn't they get it?

He had a gift, Sam acknowledged, and she knew it wasn't anything he could teach others.

"...know him, Samantha..." She quickly tuned back into Mr. Hennesey. "...so I'm putting you in charge of organizing the training sessions with Josh."

No. No, no, no, no.

"Start with personnel here this week, then bring in the others from the eastern region."

Nooooo. Except this was *exactly* the type of job the east coast manager would do. She should be thrilled that she'd been given the opportunity to prove what she could do and not one of the other candidates.

Except now she owed Josh.

"See to it that he has everything he needs," Mr. Hennesey instructed expansively.

Josh's eyes gleamed.

"He means equipment," Sam snapped.

"My equipment is just fine." He grinned. "Some have said it's the best they've ever seen."

"Then they haven't seen much."

Josh let her words hang in the air. "And you have, of course."

How was it possible to loathe a human being as much as she loathed Josh? Belatedly conscious of Mr. Hennesey's gaze ping-ponging between them, Sam once again prepared to salvage the situation. Turning to the man she hoped would become her permanent boss, she explained, "I've always made it a point to be familiar with the audio visual inventory of the hotels I recommend to organizations' meeting planners. Carrington can be justifiably proud of owning and maintaining first-rate AV equipment."

To Josh, she added, "As a start-up company it would be understandable if *your* equipment was...lacking."

Their gazes locked.

Sam could see the muscle work in Josh's temple and was silently congratulating herself for finally getting to him, when he spoke, "Bill, if you can spare Sam for a couple of hours, I'd like to show her my equipment."

3

OH, THE LOOK ON HER FACE. Nobody, but nobody, could speak with her eyes like Sam Baldwin.

They flashed. They narrowed. They stared. They blinked. And once there'd been a time when they'd gone all smoky and dark...but it was better that he forget about that. With Hennesey's blessings echoing behind them, Josh followed her from the room.

Yeah, the only downside to quitting Meckler to strike out on his own was the thought that he'd never go head-to-head with Samantha Baldwin again. Josh wouldn't mind going body to body, either. At one time, it looked like that was going to happen, *was* happening, actually, and if he hadn't had an attack of latent ethics...but he had. Surprised the hell out of him, too.

She headed for the bank of elevators and pressed— stabbed—the button, then stood silently and stared straight ahead.

Fine. He'd just wait her out. He shoved his hands into his pockets and watched her face in the reflection of the brass elevator doors.

She was doing the same, he saw. Once, again, he was struck by the expressiveness of her eyes. Like right now, they were saying, "You are a complete jerk, you know that?"

Well, sure. He didn't want to do anything halfway—
no, wait, she had actually *said* that. Out loud. He might
have gone too far this time.

Nah. "Hey, you missed your line," he said as they
got into the elevator. "When I offered to show you my
equipment, you should have said, 'Only if you're up to
it.' Or, no! You could have said, 'I'll show you mine if
you show me yours.'"

"Did I mention the jerkish aspects of your personality?" She pressed the button for the fourth floor.

"Yeah."

"And I have before, haven't I?"

"Several times. But you change the adjectives. I don't
recall you using 'complete' before. Total jerk, you've
used that. Let's see…stupid jerk. Slimy jerk. Unethical
jerk. And *such* a jerk as in 'You are *such* a jerk, Josh.'"

She narrowed her eyes. "Jerk."

"Hey an unadorned jerk! Or would that be a *naked*
jerk?" He raised his eyebrows suggestively.

Her eyes got big and her nostrils may have even
flared. He really shouldn't enjoy pushing her buttons
so much, except that they were such cute buttons.

A couple of them seem to have disconnected,
though. Sam wasn't reacting with the banked passion
she usually did. The ole you're-not-going-to-get-to-me
was missing. Sure, she was putting up a show, but her
heart wasn't in it. Maybe it was because they were no
longer competing to land conventions for their respective hotels.

He'd miss that.

She had added some much needed zing to his life the

past few months, the kind of zing a man shouldn't go too long without.

The elevator reached the fourth floor but Sam stopped the doors from opening. She drew a deep breath and slipped on her professional mask.

Uh-oh. Fun was over.

"As I understand it, we are no longer competitors."

He shook his head, unable to prevent a wistful half smile.

"I'm here in New York because three of us are being considered for the job of Carrington's convention manager for the east coast."

He'd heard something to that effect. He'd even put in a mildly good word for her, not that he'd ever admit it. "Congrats."

"Again, three of us. I want this job. It's important to me, Josh, and I would appreciate it if you...would *behave*." She ground out the last bit without looking at him, clearly hating to ask *anything* of him.

If he had a conscience, it might have twinged.

And then she turned her head and looked at him. Straight at him, her eyes...he wouldn't go so far as to say *pleading* but they were vulnerable. Definitely vulnerable.

It was a new look for her and it rattled him. Sam was as tough as they came. She played to win and when she did, she didn't gloat, and if she didn't, there was no pouting. He liked her, genuinely liked her, though he knew she'd be surprised to know it.

"Well?" She looked away and stared straight ahead.

"Sure," Josh said gruffly.

"Thanks." She released the doors and strode out,

any hint of softness now buried beneath a sternly professional outer shell.

Josh resisted the urge to mimic her straight-backed
posture. She sure wasn't going to be as much fun if she
got this job.

They walked along a wide hallway that was open to
the atrium lobby below. Though he'd never been in
this hotel before, Josh was intimately familiar with
standard hotel layout and knew the ballrooms and
meeting rooms were on this floor. "So who's your competition?"

He didn't think she was going to answer him, but finally offered, "Leonard Sheffield—"

"I know him. He's a wienie. Don't worry about
him."

"And Harvey Wannerstein."

Figured. Josh had run across him, too. Talk about
your jerks. He said nothing because it didn't look good
for Sam. She was too much of a rule follower and it
made her predictable and thus easy to outmaneuver—
like playing poker with someone who showed you her
hand. Harvey played with marked cards in mirrored
rooms with aces up his sleeve.

"Josh?"

"Hmm?"

"You've got to know Harvey. He's based here in
New York."

"Yeah. I know him."

"So what do you think?"

He looked down at her—not far, since Sam was on
the tall side. He couldn't help remembering that she fit
ever so nicely against him. "Watch your back." And a

lovely back it was, too. He considered offering to watch it for her.

"Why?"

"He's worse than me."

"I didn't think that was possible."

She walked on, but Josh stopped, right there on the muted gray-blue carpet with intarsia border. Sam would no doubt be surprised to know that *he* had buttons and that she'd just pushed one of them.

She kept walking until, all at once, she pivoted. *"What?"*

Josh drew his hands to his waist and stood firm in the middle of the hall. "I am not worse than Harvey Wannerstein. In fact, I don't like being compared to Harvey Wannerstein."

Sam took a few steps back in his direction. *"You* compared yourself to him."

"Because there are similarities in our approach—"

"You mean he beats you at your own game?"

"I mean he changes the rules after you've signed on."

She raised an eyebrow, her face the picture of contempt.

He couldn't stand it. His mother had given him that same look every time she said, "You're going to grow up and be just like your father—all talk and nothing behind it." And if there was one thing Josh didn't want, it was to look at Samantha Baldwin and be reminded of his mother. "When I make a deal, no matter how it comes about, once we shake hands, I deliver. No tricks and no gotchas. And I *never* go into a deal promising something that isn't going to happen."

Sam crossed her arms across her chest and gave him a disgusted look. "Federated Nurses, 1998."

Remembering that spectacular mess, Josh felt his face heat. She *would* bring up that. "Construction ran behind schedule and the hotel wasn't finished. I *personally* negotiated a deal with, as I recall, Carrington, on that group's behalf. And, yes, it was more than the nurses wanted to pay, but less than if they'd gone out and tried to find another hotel on their own. I did *not*—" he jabbed a finger for emphasis "—just tell them too bad, those are the breaks and send back their contract!"

"You're shouting."

He was. "I'm enunciating clearly across the chasm that divides us." Josh took a deep breath to calm down.

Looking at the toes of her shoes, Sam traced the design in the carpet and by doing so, slowly drew closer to him without giving the impression of losing ground. Atta girl.

He consciously lowered his voice. "I guess I'll have to say I don't *knowingly* promise what I can't deliver—unlike your friend Harvey."

"He's not my friend."

"Glad to hear it."

She looked up at him. "What do you know?"

Josh debated—but not for very long—on what to tell her. "I know that he has a rep for changing contract terms close to the meeting date."

"He can't." Sam shook her head. "That's why it's called a contract. That's why there are cancellation clauses and penalties."

She just wouldn't think outside the rules' box. Josh mimed making a phone call. "Federated Nurses?

About your 1998 convention, are you still predicting a thousand attendees? You are. I'm afraid there's a problem on this end. The begonia growers need to change their convention date to the weekend you wanted. They always book three thousand, so we certainly want to accommodate them. Now, if you were guaranteeing even two thousand, I could make a case for you, but I already made you a spectacular deal on the room rates. I know we were the lowest and frankly, there were a few grumbles on this end, so now the board is looking at the profit bottom line, and, well, heh, heh, begonias are just more profitable than nurses. What? Yes, even with the cancellation penalty, which we will certainly pay...no, I'm afraid we can't cover the cost of reprinting your brochures...well, I could try...if you were willing to renegotiate the contract to make it more attractive—"

"Oh, come on! Ever consider stand-up comedy?" She was still several feet away.

For a reason he didn't want to examine, Josh wanted her to think better of him than that scuz Harvey. "I wasn't trying to be funny."

"Good, 'cause you weren't."

"I'm telling you, the guy pulls this stuff all the time. Then the group renegotiates for higher rates because they don't have the time to find another hotel and it would cost a heck of a lot more if they did—even when they're paid the penalty according to the contract."

She didn't look impressed. "Somebody would have sued by now."

"How do you know they haven't? Harvey may not have been with Carrington long enough. I remember when he was with Peabody Hotels and Smith-Hunter before that. Besides, do you think he'd pull that stunt on a group that was likely to sue?"

"I think this sounds like sour grapes on your part." Sam dropped her arms, turned around, and started walking.

She didn't believe him!

"Hey!" He jogged to catch up and stopped right in front of her.

Sam stepped to one side and so did Josh. Then, predictably, she went for the other side and he blocked her there, too.

Clearly exasperated, she looked up at him.

This was the closest he'd been to her since...since the Time That Must Be Forgotten. Except he couldn't forget it.

She'd been new on the circuit. He'd run into her a couple of times before, but this time, they were on his home turf of Chicago. He was feeling expansive; she was pretty and responsive and _there,_ and instead of keeping things his usual cool and light, he'd let them get hot and heavy. When he realized what he'd done, he'd cooled things off with an uncharacteristic lack of finesse, but he _had_ cooled them.

Like straight into ice cube city.

"_What_ is it?" Ms. Icicle froze off each word.

Very quietly, very firmly Josh responded, "Harvey Wannerstein is dishonorable." It was an old-fashioned word that shouldn't be old-fashioned, to Josh's way of thinking.

She blinked. "So you've intimated."

"And I am not."

Sam rolled her eyes. "Oh, for—"

"I'm *not*." He held her gaze—once she stopped rolling her eyes.

"No, you're tricky and slick and underhanded and devious—"

"That's shrewd, suave, discreet and clever, but above all, when I give my word, I keep it. So don't think dealing with him is anything like dealing with me."

They stood there in the deserted hallway staring at each other and as far as Josh was concerned, they'd stay there all day if that's what it took. Normally he didn't care what the competition thought of him, but Sam was different. He'd rather she hated him than look at him with contempt.

As she studied him, he was having a couple of second thoughts concerning some of his more creative deals and how they might appear to someone as strait-laced as Sam, when she took a step forward and cuffed him on the shoulder.

"I believe you, you big jerk."

He grinned with a lot more relief than he wanted to admit. "Now don't go all mushy on me."

"Not a chance."

What a woman. He fought an intense urge to haul her to him and lay one on her. It would be worth the inevitable smack to his jaw. He could manage quite a kiss in the few seconds that surprise would hold her still.

But he didn't kiss her. "Remember what I said about Wannerstein."

"Yeah. Thanks."

They walked, side by side, to the Riviera Ballroom.

Sam went to the house phone sitting on a sofa table next to the wall. As she spoke into it, Josh opened the ballroom doors.

The place was impressively huge. The thought of it filled with industry professionals who were there to hear him share his knowledge gave Josh an immense feeling of satisfaction. He'd worked hard and now he was being acknowledged as the best.

"If you've started a company, then where is it? Your sisters have an office at a law firm. I can go there."

"People don't come to me. I go to them."

"You actually expect people to pay to hear what you have to say? This sounds like one of your father's slick schemes."

If he could get his mother out of his head, he could sure enjoy his success a lot more. That conversation had taken place just after Carrington had hired him on Wednesday. He didn't know why he bothered with her. She'd made up her mind about him long ago and she wasn't about to change it.

Maybe Sam had, too.

"I think I'll put you in the Barcelona Ballroom." Sam flipped on the outer square of ceiling lights. "This room is way too big." She gestured for him to follow her.

Okay, so a smaller one would be filled. He still felt proud.

"The audiovisual storeroom is in the corridor on the far end. If you can use our stuff..." Josh was amused to note the briefest hesitation before she selected the word "stuff." "...it'll be more convenient than lugging your own over here."

"Sounds like a plan." Especially since, contrary to

their earlier conversation, Josh didn't own much more than a VCR and an overhead projector. He'd always liked to travel light.

They headed across the cavernous ballroom. Sam was wearing a blouse and plain skirt in a beige color. In fact, the color reminded him of the color of her skin in muted light. Which reminded him that he'd seen quite a bit—though not all of it—in said muted light. He'd felt even more of it. Stroked it. Caressed it.

Kissed it.

"Is going into the seminar business something you'd been planning for a long time?" Sam asked.

Just what he needed—a verbal bucket of cold water.

It was the first time in a very long time that Sam had voluntarily spoken to him and Josh scrambled to answer. "No. Over the past few years, I was asked to train some of the Meckler staff—missing out on a couple of juicy commissions, I might add. Anyway, I liked training and I'm good at it, so I thought, hey. This is where the real money is. I'm going for it."

"Just like that?"

"Pretty much. Once you decide to make a change, why wait?"

"Well...to prepare. To set things up. Research."

He knew she was the deliberate type. Very rarely impulsive. But when she was... "I have set up. I've got matching brochures, stationery, tapes and textbooks, too."

There was a spark of interest in her eyes. "But you can't have been doing this very long."

"As a matter of fact, Carrington Hotels is my first client."

"Your first...Josh!"

"Hey, Hennesey got a discount and you know I'll do a great job because I want this gig to lead to more clients. Lots more. More clients than I can handle."

Sam laughed and something warmed in Josh's gut. She didn't laugh a lot when she was around him. He liked it and he liked what it did to her face, how the laughter revealed a feminine softness she usually hid.

That was the thing. Josh liked his women soft and feminine and girlie—all the politically incorrect traits. He liked the idea of a woman spending all afternoon at a beauty parlor making herself look pretty for him. He liked painted nails, scented skin and twinkling earlobes. He liked hairstyles that revealed the back of a woman's neck.

Sam would think a day in a salon was a waste. Her nails were short and unadorned, she wore no perfume, though he'd caught a whiff of flowery shampoo or soap on occasion, and her earlobes might gleam, but they never twinkled.

So what was it about her that attracted him?

"Then what?" she asked.

He had to think back. They'd been talking about his plans to become a seminar guru, specifically his desire to become overwhelmed by demand for his services. "Then I'll hire other trainers. I'll franchise, even. Because I, Joshua H. Crandall, intend to become very, very rich."

"Don't we all." She threw him an amused glance and pushed the bar on the double doors leading to the service corridor.

"But I'm going to." Josh finished opening the door.

"I want to become stinking rich. Filthy rich. Solid gold bathroom fixtures rich."

"Tacky rich. That sounds like you."

He grinned. "Maybe even very, very, *very* rich."

The doors shut behind them and they stood in a bare hallway decorated only in the scuff marks left by wheeled carts. Like all hotels, Carrington put its money in the areas that were visible to the public.

"So you become rich. What then? Buy your own hotel?" She spanned her hands indicating a marquee. "Crandall's Cut-Rate Convention Hotel. Imagine competing with that. Oh, the horror."

"No. No hotel. I'm going to give the money all away." He hadn't meant to tell her that.

"Yeah, right." Sam waved at a man waiting for them at the end of the hall. He waved back and unlocked the door to what Josh guessed was the audiovisual storeroom.

He didn't expect Sam to believe him and talk of it was premature, but that's what he was going to do if he became very, very, *very* rich. Well, at least he'd give away the three verys. Rich was enough for him. He just wanted to prove he could do it—to his family *and* himself. And then he wanted the fun of giving away money to causes he considered worthwhile—and no groveling allowed. He'd give it away all at once, so when it was gone, it was gone.

It was a lovely little fantasy which actually had a good chance of becoming reality as long as Josh didn't get sidetracked by a too-serious brunette with speaking eyes.

THIS COULD NOT BE Josh Crandall. The man standing beside her—actually peering over her shoulder or most likely down her blouse—could not be Josh Crandall. This man was acting like a human being. A decent human being. Unless he *was* looking down her blouse, but no, he seemed to be completely engrossed in the overhead projectors, thus retaining the decent label.

And earlier... Sam suppressed a shudder. Earlier while standing in the hallway, he'd metamorphosed from the loose-limbed, easygoing, aw-shucks, why-play-by-the-rules kind of guy to a...well, a man. And not just any man. A man with a firm jaw and a steely eyed gaze. A man who had no hesitation in letting a woman know he was a man and thereby making her feel very...womanly. A strong man, master of any situation.

Master of any woman.

Sam had stared him right in the eyes and just flat forgot who he was. As he'd stood there and talked of honor and dishonor, practically growing his own halo, she'd felt *very* womanly and *very* attracted to him. He could sweep her off her feet, literally and figuratively. And she had to admit—but only to herself—that the literal part had a lot of appeal.

Therefore, he couldn't be Josh Crandall. Nope. Not at all.

She'd talked to him, thinking that he'd trip up and turn back into the Josh of old, but, no, he'd shared his goals with her and she could feel herself caught up in them and even believing that he *would* give all his money away. She wanted to help him make that money, which was probably exactly what he wanted and which was so stupid, she couldn't believe she'd fallen for his story even for a minute.

It was a joke. A trick. He was up to something. Hadn't she fallen for his faux charm once before?

Even now, just at the memory, Sam's face heated and her stomach roiled. He'd been using her and the situation was such a cliché, that she figured it couldn't actually be the way it looked. It had looked like he was seducing her so that she would let him win the convention for his hotel. But Sam had thought his feelings were genuine. Instead, he actually *had* been seducing her so that he could win the convention for his hotel.

Disaster had been averted, but not by her actions.

She needed to remember the humiliation, to draw on it to counter this suspiciously appealing image he'd presented to her.

And she needed a clear head to figure out just exactly what Josh Crandall was up to now.

4

THE TAXI STOPPED IN front of The Willoughby, Sam's brand-new temporary, probably illegal sublet. Home sweet home. She hoped.

After setting on the curb a box containing a Sacher torte that was missing only two slices, Sam dragged her suitcases and a satchel from the taxi. She hoped no one stepped on tonight's dessert. Where was the so-called doorman?

Keeping a watch out for dogs with a yen for chocolate, Sam paid a taxi driver for the second time that day.

Accompanied by the blare of horns—and just what did they expect her to do?—Sam wrestled everything to the sidewalk, piggybacked the suitcases and extended the handle so she could roll them. She squinted through The Willoughby's plate-glass door, but it had been coated with a dark film to cut down on the sun's heat and she couldn't see inside.

Franco whatshisname must not be angling for much of a Christmas bonus if he wouldn't come to her rescue. Not that she'd be here at Christmas, which he no doubt had taken into consideration.

Rolling her suitcases, Sam attempted to keep the dessert box level as she elbowed the door open herself.

Franco, now dressed in jeans and T-shirt, sat on a chair reading aloud from a stack of typed pages.

Sam looked closer. A script. He was reading a script. She had struggled with luggage and chocolate and he ignored her to read a script. "Some doorman you are," she grumbled, kicking at the door so she could pull her suitcases the rest of the way inside before it closed.

"I am an actor. I'm only temporarily a doorman."

"I hope you're a better actor than you are a doorman, or you aren't going to have much of a career."

"Snippy, snippy." He closed the script and opened a steno notebook. "I am a doorman to tenants."

"That's what I'm going to be as soon as I unpack."

"You aren't a tenant, you're Tavish's guest."

"Tavish's *paying* gu—"

"La la la." Franco stuck his fingers in his ears. "I can't hear you."

She *so* didn't need this today. Sam glared at him and noticed that the sleeves on his T-shirt had ridden up to reveal a tattoo of...a blob. A furry blob.

He followed her gaze and took his fingers out of his ears. "Toto. I'm a big *Wizard of Oz* fan. Judy Garland was a goddess." As he spoke, he accompanied himself with broad, theatrical gestures. "Let me hear you say it."

"Say what? There's no place like home?"

"Well, that will do, though I really was hoping for an acknowledgment of Judy's goddess status. Now. As far as I'm concerned, you and the lovely ladies are Tavish's summer guests."

"Okay." Whatever. Sam eyed him warily.

"What? You've never seen someone out of the closet before?"

And that settled that. "I'm from San Francisco. There are no closets there."

He nodded. "A paradise on earth. What are you doing here in New York?"

Other than yanking her arm out of its socket and melting the icing on a perfectly good, but slightly used Sacher torte? She'd better humor him. Doormen could make her life miserable, she'd heard. "I work for Carrington Hotels in their meeting planner division. I'm hoping to be promoted to manager of the east coast."

"A hotel..." Franco wrote furiously and with a great many underlinings and flourishes. He was at one with the pencil. "So Tavish has sub— uh, invited an anthropologist who's researching something about people in nightclubs, a lawyer who could come across a juicy divorce, and a hotel executive. Hmm." He studied his notes, his smile growing.

Hotel executive. She might just forgive him for being a lackadaisical doorman. A.J. was the lawyer, Sam knew, so that left Claire as the anthropologist. She never would have figured Claire for an anthropologist, not that she'd ever met one. Maybe Claire could give her some tips about handling Josh.

"*Fabulous.*" Franco tapped the pencil against the notebook. "There is potential for a high gossip quotient here. What's your name?"

"Sam Baldwin."

"Sa-man-tha..." he said as he wrote.

"I prefer Sam."

"Oooo." He gave her a look, erased the rest of her

name and underlined what was left. "Do you have any gossip?"

Sam doubted he'd be interested in Josh's opinion of Harvey Wannerstein. "What kind of gossip?"

"Hon, don't you read *W* or *Vanity Fair*?"

Sam shook her head.

He gasped and rolled his eyes theatrically. "Not that I'm surprised with you in that color. I'll lend you my copies."

Sam looked down at her corporate-beige, fake linen suit. Yes, this was New York, but did she have to wear black *every* day? "What's wrong with this color?"

"There's so much of it, for one thing." He waggled his fingers. "You need a little contrast color to make your eyes pop."

"I'm not sure I want my eyes popping."

Again with his eyes rolling, Franco scribbled more. "I'll have Rocky come do your colors. For that matter, all of you need your colors done."

"Did Rocky do Tavish's colors?"

"Tavish..." He gave a long-suffering sigh. "Tavish remains a fashion maverick."

He could say that again. Sam's arm was beginning to hurt. She gestured toward the elevator. "Nice chatting with you, but I've got part of dinner with me."

"Yes, you're having Chinese tonight. So predictable. I suggested a little Greek place, but did anyone listen to me? No. After all, who am I but someone who has lived in this area for..."

During his monologue, Sam had rolled her luggage toward the elevator.

"Are you sure you don't have any gossip?" Franco called after her plaintively.

Actually... "There's an actress who always registers under the name of Mrs. McGrath. She's staying at the hotel this week." And that was all he was getting out of her.

Franco's face transformed into a delighted "O." "Monica Marbury is in town?" To Sam's horror, he whipped out a cell phone. "She must be talking to Bernard Diaz about playing Josephine in *Napoleon's Main Squeeze*."

How had he recognized the name? Sam never would have said anything if she thought there was the slightest chance that he would have known that Monica Marbury used the Mrs. McGrath alias. That was violating the hotel's strict privacy policy. She felt queasy. "Franco, you can't reveal your source."

He mimed zipping his mouth closed and throwing away the key. The elevator doors opened and Sam got inside. "I'm serious, Franco," she called.

"Oh, hon, I'll be discreet." He blew her a kiss. "And *thank* you—Rocky! Guess who's in town—"

Sam slumped against the doors as the elevator chugged its way to the sixth floor. She never, never, *never* violated hotel policy. And the one time... This was going to come back and haunt her. She just knew it.

It would have to get in line. She was currently being haunted by thoughts of Josh, or Josh in his current incarnation. He was looking mighty good in his current incarnation, of which he was most assuredly aware.

After Josh had decided to use Carrington's audiovisual equipment, they'd had a very productive meeting, surprisingly enough. His seminars would begin the middle of the following week.

He behaved perfectly, but of course there was no one else around. Still, now that they weren't on opposite sides of the negotiating table, Sam could appreciate his focus and his make-it-happen attitude. And, yes, it was attractive. She liked mature men. Mature, not older. A hard worker who was through playing juvenile games.

Was Josh through playing juvenile games? Not that she cared one way or the other.

Still. A couple of times, she'd caught him looking at her and she'd intuitively known his mind wasn't totally on setting up his seminars. Sam suspected he was remembering a certain night in Chicago and she would do well to remember it, too. Not the physical details, which she could admit had been very...pleasant and pleasant was as far as she'd go. No, she was going to concentrate on her utterly mortifying realization that once Josh knew she was seducible, he was no longer interested.

So maybe now he was interested again. She knew that look. She'd seen it in men's eyes before and she'd countered it with the same blank, nonresponsive stare she'd used on hotel execs in the past.

Josh might be interested, but she wasn't. Definitely not. And she made sure he knew it.

She sighed. Not that he'd paid any attention.

The elevator—slow as it was—eventually chugged and lurched its way to the sixth floor and Sam got out, rolling her luggage down the hall to *her* apartment. Her *apartment*.

Only she had to knock on the door, since she didn't have a key yet. A.J. was having keys made for all of them.

However, before she could knock, the door of apartment 6B across the hall opened. Standing in the doorway was a very imposing, very pastel woman.

"Oh, there you are." The woman's chiffon caftan, swirled in tones of pink and yellow, rippled from the movement of the door. Matching pink and yellow bows nested in the crown of bouffant white hair that had been tinted the palest shade of pink.

Pale or not, it was still pink.

"Tavish told me to expect not one, not two, but three healthy young things. I'm so glad." She trilled her *r*'s.

Sam had never heard anyone do that in person before.

"I'm Mrs. Higgenbotham." She extended her hand. A huge square diamond ring dominated her fingers.

For a moment, Sam wondered if she was supposed to kiss it, but Mrs. Higgenbotham merely squeezed her fingertips and raised her eyebrows expectantly.

"Oh. I'm Sam Baldwin."

"Sam? Is there more?"

"It's short for Samantha, but I really prefer—"

"Samaaaantha, this is Cleo."

Sam looked around but didn't see anyone. Mrs. Higgenbotham swooped down and picked up a curly pink...poodle. As she nuzzled the dog, Sam saw that the dog's hair and Mrs. Higgenbotham's matched.

"Cleo prefers her walksies prior to eight-thirty in the morning." Cleo licked Mrs. Higgenbotham's chin and wiggled. After practically jumping out of her arms, the dog took off into the apartment, toenails clicking on the wooden floor. "And don't forget her appointment on Thursday." With a "Mommy's coming, sweetums!" Mrs. Higgenbotham swirled back into her apartment.

Okay. Sam drew a breath of floral-scented air. Always nice to meet the neighbors.

Before she could knock on the door to her apartment, Claire opened the door and beamed. "Sam!" She grabbed for Sam's satchel. "We thought we heard you talking to Mrs. H. Anyway, A.J. brought food. Come on in. We've been waiting for you."

Sam followed her into the faux Southwest desert cowboy apartment and looked at the two women she'd never met in her life before today.

"You met the poodle lady?" A.J. asked.

"Oh, yeah. Any other neighbors I should know about?"

A.J. looked at Claire, who said, "Just my friend, Petra. She's in the apartment next to us, but she's in Bermuda right now."

A.J. smothered a smile. "Tell Sam what Petra does, Claire."

"She's a sculptress."

"And tell Sam what Petra sculpts, Claire."

Claire looked defensive. "Men."

"Tell Sam what kind of—"

"Nudes!" an exasperated Claire snapped. "She sculpts naked men, okay?"

"Okay, with me," Sam said.

"I certainly have no objection," A.J. added.

And as they all looked at each other and laughed, Sam knew she was home.

AN HOUR AND TWO SLICES OF sinfully rich chocolate dessert later, Sam and her roommates felt comfortable enough with each other to bond over the telling of relationship wars. There seemed to be a truce, since nobody was currently involved with anyone. Therefore, since Sam's antagonistic acquaintance with Josh was the nearest thing to a relationship, they decided to dissect that.

Sam was glad. Josh needed a good dissecting, preferably with a dull blade.

"So you two had a thing." Using chopsticks, A.J. put another tiny sliver of chocolate in her mouth.

They had eaten dinner sitting on the floor around a coffee table that was a square of glass atop an iron cactus. They were careful to watch out for the spikes.

"Not a 'thing.' More like a mistake. A *potential* mistake." Not nearly as elegant as A.J., Sam stuffed a whole chunk of the rich chocolate cake in her mouth.

"Who called a halt?" Claire asked.

Sam didn't know them as well as all that. Did she really want to reveal one of her most humiliating moments? Oh, why not. "He did," she mumbled around her mouthful of chocolate.

"Oooo," both roommates groaned in sympathy.

Immediately, Sam felt better. She'd never been able to discuss what had happened with anyone. Her sisters were caught up in their own lives and her mother would have hired a lawyer and instigated a sexual harassment lawsuit within twenty-four hours.

"I thought..." Sam sighed. "I knew better, but I still fell for his come-on. I thought he was on the level. You have to understand that it's very easy to like Josh, even when you know he's slick and tricky and as shallow as a soup plate. Let me tell you about the MOO convention."

"Moo?" Claire asked.

"Midwestern Orthodontists Organization. This was after our...thing. I was determined to show him that I'd forgotten all about that night. And I wanted to win that convention more than anything and I was going to do it by being the best. And I was the best. But they didn't choose Carrington."

"Why not?" Claire asked.

Of her two roommates, Claire looked the most sympathetic. A.J. didn't look as though she'd *ever* fall for a slick charmer like Josh.

"There was a pending patent infringement case against MOO's president, so I knew he didn't need any more stress. I planned my proposal down to the last detail. Everything would have been taken care of for him. So guess what Josh does?"

"I don't know," A.J. said. "Brought in a girl in a cake?"

That did sound like Josh. "No. He went to the plaintiff and mediated a settlement." She looked at A.J. "Is that legal?"

"If he didn't present himself as a professional mediator, I think he was okay. I could look it up," she offered.

"Don't bother," Sam said. "It wouldn't change anything. The MOO president was very grateful. Naturally, he chose Meckler Hotels not only for that year's conference, but for the next four years and didn't quibble too much over the terms, either. So I had to go back to the Carrington Executive Board and try to explain why my proposal was turned down not only for that year, but four years in the future." She closed her eyes at the memory. "That was not fun."

"Ouch," Claire said.

"And I don't care what you said, A.J., Josh had to have done something illegal—and he got away with it! He always does. He's so..." Sam sighed again. "And I thought he really felt something for me that time."

"Maybe he did." Claire pressed her finger against her plate to pick up any stray crumbs. "Did you feel something for him?"

Yeah, but was it a true something, or had she just been caught up in the circumstances? "At the time. I despise him now."

"Hmm." Claire looked at A.J.

A.J. nodded. "You can say that again."

Sam looked from one to the other. "But what did she say?"

"You need closure," A.J. said.

"You've never resolved your feelings for him," Claire added.

"Sure I have. I've resolved to hate him."

"What did he say to you afterward?" Claire asked.

"Nothing. We never speak about it."

"There you are." A.J. resolutely closed the box on the rest of the Sacher torte. "You need to have it out with him."

Sam eyed the box longingly, but knew putting it away was for the best. "I can't. It was almost two years ago."

Both her new roommates looked at her with identical expressions of astonishment. "And he's still hanging around you?" A.J. asked.

"He's not hanging around. The meeting industry isn't that big and you keep running into the same people."

"Uh-huh." Now they were grinning at her.

"What?" Sam asked.

"Sam's got a boyfriend," Claire said in a singsong voice.

"I thought you were supposed to like your boyfriend," Sam retorted.

"Maybe you do," Claire said.

"That's the problem! He's not worth liking. He's pretending to be somebody worth liking, so I'll like him, but all he'll get is a fake like."

Claire nodded. "Believe it or not, I do understand."

"Then explain it to me," A.J. said.

"Sam needs to level the relationship. She exposed deeper emotions to him and became vulnerable. He hasn't reciprocated, so he holds the power in their relationship. He knows how she feels—"

"Felt," Sam clarified.

"How she *felt*, but she doesn't know how he feels. Felt. No, probably still feels."

"Look, in case I didn't make myself clear, he felt—feels—nothing," Sam argued. "He was just using me to get what he wanted. And he didn't want me, he wanted the organization to choose Meckler Hotels over Carrington and the others."

"But, how shall I put this..." A.J. drew a breath. "As I understand it, he didn't *finish* using you."

"No." Sam gazed into the middle distance. "He didn't."

"The solution is simple," Claire offered. "Sam needs to get him all hot and bothered, then leave *him* high and dry. Then their relationship—"

"I don't have a—"

"Yes, you do," Claire insisted. "Then when you get him to reveal himself at an equal emotional depth and spurn—"

"I like that word 'spurn,'" A.J. interrupted.

"Stop it and let me finish!" Claire looked stern, or as stern as the petite woman with the big eyes could. "Sam has to get him the same way he got her, then things will be equal between them again. What they do after that is up to them."

"Claire, I'm so impressed." A.J. applauded. "And you learned all this by being an anthropologist?"

"No, I learned it by being a woman."

"Right on, sister."

"You know, Claire's right." Sam liked the idea of Josh begging for her and hearing her say, "We both know this isn't a good idea." And then he'd say, "I won't tell if you won't." And she'd say, "You're so hot and so tempting, but you aren't worth my job, babe."

She'd be sure she said "babe."

Then she'd walk away. Strut away, actually. She had to remember that part, otherwise the whole scenario wouldn't work.

She imagined his hotel room. Josh never settled for the freebies or the unrentable rooms. Somehow, he ended up in a junior suite, at least.

So, there would be a sofa. That was important since

the Chicago incident had occurred on a sofa. And some lingering kisses—the slow, deep kind at which Josh excelled. That was important, too. Josh needed plenty of time to reacquaint himself with her mouth...the way she tasted...the way she felt beneath his hands...

"You know," Sam admitted in a small voice. "The walking away part might not be so easy."

"Sam!" The other two exclaimed in unison.

"Wear that skirt you wore for Tavish," A.J. added.

"Yeah. It turned him and the two brokers into zombies."

"It did, didn't it?" Sam thought of it on the closet shelf. "I don't know...men act weird around it."

Claire and A.J. looked at each other. "Ask her," Claire said.

"You told us that it originally came from some island and had a special thread woven into the material and that it would attract men, one of whom would be your true love," A.J. began. "But how did you get it?"

"I caught it at a wedding." Actually, it was more like the skirt had caught her. "That's how it's passed from one woman to the next."

A.J. got up and put the dessert box in the fridge. "So, like, you're the only one it'll work for?"

"I don't know...that wasn't part of the legend I was told." Sam smiled at them. "You two want to borrow it and see if it works for you?"

"Could we?" Claire looked as though she was ready to change into it right then.

"Fine with me."

"The funny thing is, I've got a skirt that looks just

like it." A.J. disappeared into her bedroom and quickly came back with a black skirt.

Sam smothered a smile. Clearly, her roommates had been discussing the skirt. "The bridesmaids were wearing them at the wedding, too. I think there was a magazine article about the whole thing a few months ago. Maybe you can find out more about it."

"I'll do that," A.J. said.

Claire shook her head. "I can't believe you're so casual about it."

"Well...it doesn't look like much. I'll go get it." Sam headed for her bedroom and took the skirt off the closet shelf. She hadn't unpacked yet, so it was the only thing in the closet.

The instant her hands touched the fabric, she was again conscious of its sumptuous weight. Impulsively, she took off her beige skirt and put on the black one.

There was a full-length mirror on the inside of the closet door. Sam looked at herself in the skirt. She looked like a woman wearing a beige blouse and a black skirt. Nothing extraordinary.

Shrugging, she joined the others. "What do you think?" she asked them.

They studied it, touching the fabric and looking at the thing from all angles.

"I don't know," A.J. said doubtfully. "Is it see-through?"

Sam walked across the room to the modest kitchen. "Well?"

Claire squinted. "I don't *think* it is. What do men see that we don't?"

A.J. just shook her head. "I have no idea."

"I don't either, but..." Sam gestured all around them. "...it got us this apartment."

"True," A.J. said. "Clearly, it's a guy thing."

"Uh-huh." Claire nodded.

They both kept staring at it and made Sam feel strange. She started for the bedroom to change out of the skirt. "So, if you two want to borrow it, that's okay with me. Just let me know first."

Because eventually, Sam decided, Josh and the skirt were going to have to meet.

She could hardly wait.

5

"FIND OUT ALL YOU CAN about potential customers because your first act on meeting a prospect is to comment on something you both have in common. You have to make a connection and bond in some way. The instant you do, he'll have invested emotionally in the encounter. Once he's done that, he—and I am also referring to the fairer sex—won't be as willing to walk away."

Sam almost broke her pencil in two. *The fairer sex. Could* Josh be more offensive?

Granted, most of the Carrington personnel here to listen to him were male, but he didn't have to make such an issue of it. Sam was thinking that she might make an issue of it when she got her promotion, but that was for another time.

Today was the first time she'd seen Josh in over a week, though she'd been the recipient of several breezy phone calls, which she'd found mildly pleasant. So, he gave good phone. That didn't come as any surprise.

What did come as a surprise was Hennesey informing her and the other candidates that they had to attend Josh's seminar. Sam had tried—unsuccessfully—not to feel offended. She told herself that, logically, she should know the content of Josh's lectures if she wanted to hire him in the future. That had to be the reason.

So Sam had been sitting here since nine o'clock this morning. Harvey Wannerstein had slipped out during the lunch break. Leonard Sheffield, the other candidate, sat on the front row assiduously taking notes.

So what should she do? Harvey's defection implied that he believed he was more advanced than the material. It made him look strong. But Hennesey wanted them to be there. Harvey could have a legitimate reason for missing the afternoon session, though if he did, Sam was sure it was self-serving.

Leonard might be preparing an analysis of the seminar. Should Sam be prepared to do likewise? Or maybe this material was all new to Leonard.

Sam rolled her eyes. Like Josh had mentioned anything she didn't already know. Whatever magic he had, he wasn't sharing it with the group.

Sam hadn't expected him to. He couldn't. Josh's charisma couldn't be taught. His techniques could, but so far, nothing Sam had heard was earth-shattering or anything a motivated newcomer wouldn't pick up after a few months in the field as she had.

The part she needed help on was dealing with cutthroat competitors and their sneaky undermining tricks. Dealing with people like, oh, Josh for instance.

Smiling to herself, she took the three-by-five card on which participants were supposed to ask questions and wrote. Then she held up the card and the meeting monitor collected it to take to Josh.

JOSH SAW THE MONITOR pick up the card from Sam. He'd been aware of everything about her all day. He knew when she smiled, not often, when she made a note, rarely, and when she stared at him, constantly.

He couldn't think why she was here except to razz him, but she hadn't yet. He'd seen Wannerstein leave and had mentally rolled his eyes at Sheffield's obvious sucking up. But what was Sam's angle?

What had she written on the card? Maybe it was just an invitation to dinner.

Or maybe it was a pithy statement invalidating everything he'd said up until now.

Waiting for her to make her move had preoccupied Josh and more than once, he'd lost his place in his prepared patter. Since only he knew his lecture, probably no one noticed, but he'd rehearsed until he could recite the script in his sleep and faltering got on his nerves.

Sam got on his nerves, too, and she knew it. She sat there, legs crossed, swinging her foot. It was the only regular movement in the room and constantly drew his attention.

That and her leg. Today, she'd worn a skirt on purpose. She had those long legs and she knew how to use them. Very effectively. And Josh wasn't even a leg man. Or he hadn't been.

Josh had often thought that if she'd dressed just a little sexier—shorter, tighter skirts, for instance—she'd be unbeatable. But no, Sam was all caught up in the forget-I'm-a-woman-and-treat-me-equally stuff. As if.

Flirting was harmless and put a little fizz in people's day. Josh liberally passed out the smiles and the compliments to the women he encountered. The secretaries always took his calls and he usually got through to the people he wanted.

Sam should try it. She might like it. With that smile of hers—the one that made her face go all soft—shorter skirts and a couple of squirts of perfume, Josh would be left talking to the receptionists and Sam would be in with the boss sewing up the contract.

And, yeah, the bosses were mostly men and the receptionists were mostly women. So what? That was the way it was.

But when he did run into a female exec, watch out.

Trying to stop thinking about Sam, Josh picked up the control to the overhead projector.

"Once you've established that bond, watch the body language. I'll be covering body language interpretation in another segment, but for now, let's look at these illustrations. On the left is the salesmen. Now, check out the client. He's crossed his legs, right over left and is leaning back in his chair." Josh showed the next photo. "Notice that the salesman has adopted a similar posture. He's establishing a subliminal rapport. The client will feel comfortable with him, but, unless he's been to one of my seminars, he won't know why."

He glanced out at the audience. Now what was she doing? Sam had picked up her pamphlet and was lazily fanning herself, like a Southern belle in her porch swing on a summer Sunday afternoon. She was slouched backward in the chair. Exactly like the illustration on Josh's slide, as a matter of fact.

Well, not exactly. The man in the photo wasn't pulling at the neckline of his shirt or piling his hair on top of his head as he fanned himself with a Perfect Pitch brochure. The man in the photo wasn't making him sweat.

And it wasn't even hot in the room. Though now that she'd brought it to his attention, it did seem a trifle warm.

Within moments a couple of others had begun to fan themselves.

She'd done that intentionally, he realized. It illustrated his point about matching body language, but nobody was likely to pick up on it.

She was clever.

He wished she'd go away.

She kept staring at him with a bored expression. Well, of course she was bored. This was beginner stuff. She didn't need to be here. He'd get into advanced techniques later on. She didn't need those either.

Unless...unless she was here to evaluate him. Of course. That was it.

Josh's heart rate sped up. This was his first full-fledged seminar. He had to nail it so that he could use Carrington as a reference. He wanted industry word of mouth. He wanted everyone in this room to go forth and sell.

He wanted Sam to just go.

He began to second-guess everything he said. Was the material *too* elementary? Was he boring? When was the last time anyone laughed at one of his jokes?

Were they learning *anything*?

As Josh kept lecturing, he felt beads of sweat gather in his armpits and run down his sides. Old-fashioned nervous sweat.

And all due to the siren with the long legs who was

currently leaning forward, chin in hand, revealing the V of her blouse. Josh could imagine what was down that V. Not an exact image though. Close, but he had to use his imagination on some pertinent places because when he'd had the opportunity, he hadn't used anything else. Yeah, he'd unhooked her bra to reach the old pertinents and she'd breathed a sigh—a soft, surrendering, quiver-at-the-end, *feminine* sigh.

And that was the end of it. At least for him.

Women who sighed like that were not the type to exchange cards or give him a call-me-next-time-you're-in-the-city, the next morning. They weren't going anywhere.

After hearing her sigh, Josh knew Sam didn't know the rules. He had, in fact, been surprised she'd wanted to play the game. Only he'd suddenly realized she wasn't playing games. She was playing for keeps.

No one had ever wanted to play for keeps with him before. He never gave them a chance to, he supposed. Why would he? He didn't want to keep *anything*. He leased a furnished apartment and stored a couple of boxes of stuff in his parents' attic. That was it. The rest, he kept liquid, or he didn't keep it at all.

But Sam...with all the mental energy he'd expended thinking about her in the past two years, he suspected Sam was different. He didn't want her to be different. He wanted her to be temporary like all the other people in his life who weren't related to him. People were best when they came and went and nobody got to know anybody else really well. In Josh's experience, no one improved on deeper acquaintance.

Keep it light, keep it simple, keep it shallow, that was his motto.

Involuntarily, his eyes strayed toward Sam who sat there looking very dark, very complex and very deep.

IF SHE DIDN'T KNOW better, Sam would think Josh was nervous. But she did know better and admired the way he injected his voice with a slight tremor once or twice. The nervous laughter was a nice touch, too. But wiping his hands on his trousers might have been overkill.

Josh was making himself appear vulnerable to elicit empathy from the audience. He looked earnest and sincere. If he'd employed his usual slick delivery, it wouldn't have the same resonance. By looking the tiniest bit unsure of himself, he had the audience rooting for him to succeed and thus paying attention.

Okay, maybe Sam *could* learn something from him. Vulnerability as a strength. It had never worked for her, but maybe that was because she was genuinely vulnerable and not manipulatively vulnerable the way Josh was.

Look at that. He'd actually pulled at his shirt collar. He was wearing one of his better sports coats, a light blue shirt and a tobacco-colored tie. *Wear a color that matches your eyes near your face. If you can't do that, wear blue because it evokes sincerity.* Okay, so Sam happened to know that his eyes were just that shade of brown. Hers were brown, too, but wearing brown didn't do a whole lot for her colorwise.

She knew this for a fact because Franco had forced her, A.J. and Claire to submit to having their colors done. His friend Rocky had dropped off his fabric drapes because he had a job in the chorus of *Napoleon's Main Squeeze* so Franco had waylaid them and draped colored fabrics over their shoulders each time they went in or out of the building.

If Sam heard that this or that color made her eyes "pop" one more time...

Except that he was right. According to him she was a "deep" winter so she could get away with black-brown or a brown-burgundy, but definitely no beige or camel or cream. Black and white was good for her, and the other colors were a lot brighter and more intense than she was used to wearing. And after a couple of, "Gee, have you lost weight?" remarks, she was sold.

Fortunately, she salvaged her beige fake linen suit by wearing a turquoise scarf even though she'd never been a scarf person before. To Franco, everyone was a scarf person and it truly wasn't worth arguing with him.

She felt pretty and she wasn't used to feeling pretty. Not that she was ugly, but her mother had cautioned Sam and her sisters to downplay their looks and dress conservatively to avoid being typecast as too feminine to get the job done.

She wondered if Josh thought she was pretty. Yes, he found her attractive—off and on—but pretty was different. Pretty implied a, well, feminine smallness. And while Sam liked being tall, there were times when she wanted to feel small and protected and cherished and all that other rot. At times, she kinda, sorta wanted to be the type of woman a man would carry off to the bedroom before having his way with her.

But that feeling was hidden in the deepest corner of

her soul. She periodically threw rocks at it to make sure it stayed there.

Sam cupped her chin in her hand and tried to concentrate on what Josh had been saying. He was going on about body language.

He was kind of cute, himself. Normally, she didn't think of him as cute, but standing up there, looking endearingly earnest—even though it *was* an act—well, he looked adorable. He was such a good actor.

And not a bad kisser, either.

Oh, please. Any man who doesn't immediately jam his tongue down your throat is a good kisser.

"If you find yourself in a situation where you're with a bunch of guys sitting around a conference table, spread out. You should always have pens and cards and files and brochures and, you know, lots of stuff. What you do is spread that stuff around and establish your territory. Don't poach on one of the other salesmen's space, but make sure you nail down your own."

"But..." someone began and trailed off.

Josh peered into the audience. "Len, got a question? Go ahead."

"Not a question so much as a comment," Leonard Sheffield began ponderously. "One doesn't want to appear messy and disorganized."

Boy, Sam could imagine what *his* sock drawer looked like.

"I didn't say smear it around—"

"You said spread."

"Yeah, I did." Josh walked to the edge of the platform. "Because that's what I meant. You can deliberately stake out four corners of neatly stacked materials and everybody will figure you for a rigid, stuffy and definitely unfun kind of guy." Josh let a beat go by in which everyone instantly realized that Leonard Sheffield *was* a rigid, stuffy and unfun kind of guy. "Nah, just go in there and casually dig through your briefcase and randomly set out your stuff—a little to each side and some in front of you. You now own that territory and it looks like you did it because you felt you were entitled. It makes you look relaxed and confident. The other way makes you look defensive and worried somebody might take your turf away."

"But what does it matter?"

"Selling is a mind game. You want to psych out the competition and reassure the client. And one way to check the score is to watch people's body language." Josh went back to his slides.

Nice segue, Sam thought.

"Check how the prospect in this picture is looking to the side. That means he's skeptical about what's being proposed."

There were several more slides during which Sam noticed how the light from the projector nicely haloed Josh's head.

She sat there, her own body language very open and amenable—if he cared to notice. She sighed and straightened.

"Let's go back to the conference table. No matter what you're told, the people in charge are going to sit in the central seats and do most of the talking. If you're given a choice, that's where you sit."

He changed slides. "You should work on your patter so that when you do make your presentation, you won't have any verbal stumbles. Step up the pace and keep your voice in the middle register. Sometimes when people talk faster than they're used to, their voice gets higher like this. And that's what we do when we're nervous."

He demonstrated and there were a few rueful chuckles in recognition.

"We're after energy, not nerves. Also, keep your gestures fluid and make eye contact because that's how the big kahunas do it. Now." He clapped his hands together and surveyed the audience. "My favorite part. I need some volunteers to demonstrate power techniques at the conference table."

Sam slunk down in her seat, deliberately crossed her arms and refused to make eye contact. *Read this body language, buster.*

"Ah, thank you. You two...let's get someone from this side of the room. You in the Snoopy tie—we'll talk. Come on up. Now we don't want to leave out the ladies."

Sam ducked her head.

"No volunteers? I'll just have to draft. How about our hostess from Carrington? Sam?"

Hostess. Grr. If there had been a way out, Sam would have taken it. As it was, all she could do was give a good-sport smile and walk up there to the platform and join the men around the table.

Remembering what Josh had said, two of them had good-naturedly jockeyed for the middle position. Sam sat at one end.

"So everybody can see, we're only sitting on one side." Josh, himself, took a seat at the other end.

"Ladies, I want you to see how sitting at the table is good for you because it diminishes the height advantage."

Since Sam was already as tall as some men, height had never been one of her weaknesses. She thought about pointing this out, but decided to give Josh a break.

A few moments later, Sam wanted to give him a break of a different kind.

"Let's look at what everyone is wearing, starting with Mr. Snoopy tie." Josh went around the table until he came to Sam.

She felt confident because of Franco's color analysis even though she'd left her scarf du jour in her office, along with her jacket.

"V-neck blouse. Wrong," Josh said.

Immediately, Sam could feel the eyes of every male in the room focus on her chest.

And as if that weren't enough, Josh approached her. "You see her neck dimple?"

Neck dimple? What was he talking about?

And then—and then he *touched* her throat. "Right here—this little indention at the base of the throat."

It felt as though his fingers lingered and caressed the area and there was not one thing Sam could do about it without looking embarrassed, which she was.

"Revealing this is a universal sign of weakness or surrender. It says approach, I'm harmless. All this time, you thought ties were an idea thought up by women so they'd have something to give us for Father's Day and Christmas, right?"

There was the camaraderie of male laughter as Sam desperately hoped she wasn't blushing.

"Guys, you can go the open-shirt route when you want to appear casual and nonthreatening. You ladies already have a problem showing strength, so cover up, either with a scarf, a high neck, or better yet, a wide gold choker."

Sam couldn't let that pass without a response. "Naturally, if I were making a presentation, I would have dressed differently."

Josh turned back to her. "So what signal are you trying to send today, Sam?"

She narrowed her eyes.

Josh laughed. "She just sent me a very definite negative signal using her eyes. We're going to cover the eyes last." He gave her a minisalute. "Message received, Sam."

That he was an egotistical jerk? She wondered if she'd called him that before.

"Okay, everybody, hands on the table. Guys, you need a significant watch. Make it a good one, the best you can afford—and not any of those digital wear-it-while-scuba-diving watches. Make it gold or silver. If you're married wear your wedding ring. Wear long-sleeved shirts and if you can pull off French cuffs and cuff links, so much the better. Ladies should also wear a watch, but you should wear a bracelet—not a little jangly one, but a cuff type. All these will give weight and add visibility to your gestures. Look at Sam down there. Hold up your arm, Sam."

Warily, she did so.

"She's got the cuffs, but no bracelet and a dinky little ladies' watch. Very pretty little feminine wrists."

Great. *Now* she was little and feminine. Sam put her arm down before she demonstrated just how much strength she had in her "pretty little feminine wrists." Criticizing her without giving her a chance to prepare was not fair. She wasn't a bracelet person, though. And as for her watch...it had been a graduation present from her aunt who had always been very good about seeing that Sam, the youngest of four girls, had just as much fuss made over her as her older sisters.

Josh went on having them demonstrate effective gestures to use when speaking. Sam felt on solid ground here, but Josh managed to find something to adjust with everything she did. Each adjustment involved touching her—her shoulder, her arm, her hand—outwardly benign. Possibly truly benign, except that this was Josh and he knew exactly what he was doing.

What he was doing was undermining her in front of people she'd have to supervise and she couldn't figure out a way to counter it.

And he'd promised to behave.

"One way you can check the effectiveness of your presentation is to hand your prospect a brochure. See if he takes it using what's called a 'decision grip.'" Josh handed Sam a brochure, which she tossed on the table.

"Ooo. No sale there. Also notice that she's crossed everything that can be crossed. We've got total rejection here. Good demo, Sam."

He walked around so that he was behind her. "Now let's show them a sale. I hand her a brochure..."

Sam took it and Josh immediately covered her hand

with his. Against her will, she felt the warmth, fought the awareness.

"Hold it like this. Okay, notice that she has lots of flesh touching the brochure as though she's already decided to make it her possession." Josh still held her hand. Leaning close, he crooned, "She *wants* it."

Sam deliberately brought her head back and caught Josh on the chin. "Oh! You startled me!" She said it loud enough for everyone to hear.

Josh immediately dropped her hand to rub his chin. Sam gave him a cool look.

And he winked at her.

That. Was. It. Josh Crandall was no longer cute, or endearing, or held the slightest bit of attraction for her.

As for his kisses—ha!

As for his invincible sales technique—double ha!

She was going to get him back for undermining her. Somehow.

But by the end of the lecture, Sam still hadn't come up with a plan. It had to be very public so that not only would he be professionally embarrassed, but her own superior salesmanship would be demonstrated.

She'd returned to her seat and Josh was now at the podium taking questions.

He was a hit, that was clear. She silently fumed as all the sales staff peppered him with questions, not even waiting until the written questions were answered.

She could have answered the questions, but did anybody ask her? No. And why not? Josh Crandall, that's why not. She'd been relegated to one of the audience instead of senior staff being considered for management.

Even Leonard Sheffield had come off better than she had.

"Let me go to the written questions here," Josh said, clearly pleased with his reception. He shuffled through the index cards. "Ah, answered that...and that..." He sailed them into the audience and got good-natured laughter in return.

Men. No, make that *boys*.

"Ditto." Flip. "Ditto." An underhanded Frisbee shot. "Here's one— What should be your strategy when it's obvious that you've lost the sale?" Josh shook his finger playfully. "It ain't over until the contract is signed. Seriously, make yourself look as good as possible. I know it'll be tough, but compliment the competition in front of the prospect." There were grumbles. "Hey, I said it'll be tough, but you need to say that you'd hoped you could do business, but you know that he'll be in good hands with the other guy. And if things don't work out, here's your card. Because, again, it ain't over until the contract is signed and sometimes not even then. You also want to keep the lines of communication open. Find out what the deciding factor was and address it at the next presentation."

Josh flipped the card into the audience and silently read the next question. He stared at it a moment, then read, "How can I anticipate and counter sneaky, underhanded maneuvers by competitors?"

Josh looked up from the card and straight at Sam. "By buying them a cup of coffee."

6

"THIS ISN'T WHAT I HAD IN mind." Sam banged the cup of coffee onto the stone seat surrounding the tree in the Carrington lobby atrium.

She was mad. Josh got the message. Loud and coffee-splashed clear. "It isn't what I had in mind, either. I was thinking a seat at the bar, or a corner table in the bistro, or a booth in the jazz club."

"And I was thinking you'd actually answer the question rather than blackmailing me for coffee."

Josh sipped the coffee from the lid before prying off the plastic. "This coffee isn't worth blackmail."

"It's a premium blend of our special Carrington roast. Blind tastings have demonstrated that it's on par with the leading gourmet coffee shop coffees."

She'd gone all professional on him. Angry professional. Interesting combination. But not one he wanted to explore right now.

He'd better figure out what he'd done to tick her off. He very much doubted it was the two bucks or whatever she'd spent on the coffee.

The fountains in the pools on either side of the tree changed their pattern and misted him with recycled blue-tinted water. "Such ambiance."

"This lobby is considered one of the most beautiful

in New York." Ms. Professional emptied three vanilla-flavored creamer cups into her coffee and stirred.

Josh shuddered and went with half a sugar. "What's bugging you, Sam?"

She took a long swallow, which, considering how hot the coffee was, impressed him. "You deliberately made me look foolish in front of everyone."

He'd been afraid he'd shown too much favoritism. "How?"

"How?" She gulped more coffee. "*How?* You're going to pretend you don't know?"

"Uh...yeah."

"You embarrassed me. I became the poster girl for incompetent saleswomen everywhere. Had I known you were critiquing dress, I would have worn something else."

"I've seen you wear that blouse before."

She gave him a look that dripped with disdain—or that could be the blue-tinted water. "Actually, you haven't. It's new."

"Okay, maybe not that exact blouse, but I've seen you wear a similar style."

"It's a woman's blouse, that's the way they're designed."

"With the, uh—" he gestured with his index finger "—V neckline. Those aren't good."

"You spend a lot of time looking at women's necklines, Josh?"

"Since I started researching the theories behind body language, yes. I was serious about the neck dimple."

"You made that up."

"No, but it sounds better than suprasternal notch."

He nodded toward her. "You have a nice one, by the way."

She looked away and sipped at her coffee, slower now. "Aside from that, you called my competency into question by criticizing everything I did. I'm a senior sales representative. People expect me to already know this stuff."

"Sam, you showed them that it's never too late to learn. They *admire* you for that."

She shot him a look that could have cut through steel.

People could be so touchy when accepting honest criticism. "Sam, I'm telling you, you've got great potential. You could be the best."

"*Potential?*" she whispered, but might as well have shouted. "You have the gall to sit there and tell me I have *potential?*"

"Sam..." He was overusing her name. He set his coffee cup down and used his hands for emphasis. His movements were going to be fluid and contain some truth verifying gestures, if she cared to analyze them. She probably wasn't going to.

The thing was, she did need to make some adjustments in her technique and now that he wasn't competing against her, he figured he'd use the opportunity to give her some tips. She was already mad at him, so what did he have to lose? "You're good, but you need to loosen up a little. You're aggressive and strong and know your material, but all that competence can be a little off-putting."

She didn't say anything. Just stared at him. Okay, he could deal with that. "People are intimidated. And they might choose another hotel chain just because you make them uncomfortable."

"*Men* are intimidated, you mean."

"Most of the people we deal with in our business are men, but even the women can be put off. It's because you are so strong, it makes them look weaker by comparison, so they aren't going to want you around giving people the opportunity to compare."

"They know I'm not after their job."

"You don't have to be. You're *too* good."

"You wouldn't tell a man that."

"I wouldn't have to. This isn't about gender. This is about sales psychology. Don't forget the goal." He should heed his own advice. "You want the sale. Like it or not, there are intangibles that affect the sale. *Your* sales. Some of the women don't want to work with you."

"And you know this for a fact." She spoke flatly.

Josh couldn't tell what she was thinking, but at least she appeared to be listening to him. "I've heard some talk."

"Pillow talk?"

Was that jealousy? Cool. He liked the idea of Sam being jealous. He gave her a broad smile and said nothing. Eventually Sam turned away.

"Now, Sam, you're obviously fairly successful. But your approach could stand a little tweaking."

"So I'd become more like you, in other words."

"You could do worse."

"I could do better." She stood, crumpled the cup, and tossed it toward a pebbled trash canister. It hit the rim and bounced off.

"That's my point," he said.

She held his gaze, then walked over, picked up the crumpled cup and stuffed it in the trash. "Thank you for your concern, but save it for the newbies." And she walked off.

Exhaling heavily, Josh watched her, watched the fluid line of her legs and the careful way she kept her hips from swaying. He'd lost whatever inroads he'd made with her, which was probably just as well. He liked the idea of having someone like Sam in his life— no, he meant Sam. Might as well admit it. Sam in his life would be great. She'd be a lot of fun and they could have some good times together.

Except he liked the idea of Sam more than the reality. Reality was that she was not the type of woman he wanted in his life when he was ready to have a woman in his life.

She wasn't...restful. They would constantly be butting heads over everything. He needed downtime. With Sam, there wouldn't be any.

Reality wasn't looking so hot.

Crumpling his own cup, he tossed it and landed it in the waste receptacle. "He shoots, he scores...and the crowd goes wild."

Sam didn't even look back.

SAM SAT IN THE CUBICLE she'd been assigned and took several deep breaths in an effort to force herself to breathe normally again.

She'd just been personally lectured by Josh Crandall on sales techniques after an afternoon of being publicly criticized by Josh Crandall on her sales techniques.

Josh Crandall was not her favorite person at the moment.

Sam actually started to call her mother, then stopped. She didn't need her mother's advice because she already knew what she'd say.

Sam's mother was in the first wave of feminists who raised the glass ceilings in business and intended for her daughters to keep raising them.

Her mom had even given Sam and her sisters names that could be shortened to sound like men's names. Thus Christine was Chris, Joanne became Jo, and Patricia, the oldest, was Pat.

They'd all fought the good fight, and now it was Sam's turn and she wanted to go higher than any of them.

Today, she'd lost stature. If Hennesey heard anything about the demonstration, her promotion was toast. Her mother would tell her that she had to reestablish herself and she needed something big. Something spectacular.

She needed to beat Josh at his own game.

Sam spent the next several hours—missing dinner and Claire's nouveau cuisine—poring over convention records, specifically those being held at Meckler Hotels. After nosing around in the records, Sam decided she wanted to go after one of the conventions that Josh had landed and get it for Carrington. That should squash any questions about her sales ability.

It was after eleven o'clock that night when she found an organization that would fit her purposes. The Family Values Assembly. It was a biggie because whole families attended. The board had gone with Josh and

Meckler for four years in a row. Last year, Carrington hadn't even bothered to bid.

The convention took place each June after school was out, so Sam figured the timing was right to approach them, if not for next summer, then the one after that.

She was going to land that convention for Carrington and show Josh just how much she didn't need his "help."

A WEEK LATER, SAM WAS ready. She'd wrangled a meeting with the Family Values Assembly board for Wednesday morning in Tulsa, Oklahoma. Even better, Josh was still around, giving his seminar to a different group of Carrington staff while videotaping the first group for a one-on-one analysis.

He must be costing Carrington a fortune, she thought. *I, Joshua H. Crandall, intend to become very, very rich.* It looked like he was on his way.

For now.

Sam had prepared the presentation of her life and for the finishing touch, she was going to let Franco dress her. Not literally, but she was definitely going to pay attention to his color magic. She'd even harvested the juiciest piece of gossip she could find as a reward— for which she'd had to reassign Carl, one of the bellmen, to the suites where he could get bigger tips.

And bigger gossip.

From the subway, Sam walked along the ritzy street leading to their apartment. She still couldn't believe they were living there. Still couldn't believe that when she stopped at the little grocery on their block for fruit and bottled water, she could literally rub elbows with movie stars and millionaires.

There weren't any stars in the grocery today. Sam bought some strawberries and a couple of energy bars, along with a large bottle of water to carry on the plane to Tulsa. Reaching her building, she dragged open the heavy door as usual, but instead of hurrying past Franco and whatever persona he'd chosen for the day, she stopped and assumed an air of someone who knew a secret. She expected Franco's gossip meter to buzz, but he was busy.

Sheesh. The *one* day she was packing gossip and Franco didn't ask her.

Today, he'd apparently decided he was a karate/ judo master. In full black belt outfit—yeah, right—he instructed another man. Actually he kept flinging the other man to the mat. Even though it was all fake, it looked pretty impressive.

There was a thud and a groan. "Do you think I've got a chance?" The other man squinted up at Franco from the mat.

"No."

"But, Franco!"

"It took me years to earn this!" He tugged at the belt.

"Earn?" Sam couldn't help asking.

"Yes, earn." Franco scowled, first at her, then back at the man on the mat. "And he wants me to teach him a few moves so he can land a commercial. A *commercial.*"

The other man stood. "Is she one?"

"Yeah. Rocky, this is Sam. Sam, Rocky." Franco had lost his usual eloquence.

Rocky looked her up and down. "You're right. She's a deep winter."

Ah, he was *that* Rocky. "Thanks for lending Franco your drapes. In fact, I have a favor to ask."

"Oh, get in line, hon. Get in line." Franco glared at Rocky.

"I was talking to Rocky," Sam protested mildly. "I'm giving a presentation and I want a killer outfit. I want to look strong and competent. It might involve shopping." That might be enough to induce them to help her and she could save the gossip for another time.

Rocky raised a hand. "Love to, babe, but I'm out. I've got auditions this whole week." He gathered up his stuff.

Franco was studying her with narrowed eyes and nearly missed Rocky's sudden attack. Nearly. Without even looking at his friend, Franco extended an arm and flipped him to the floor.

"Ow. Enough. I'm going." Looking aggrieved, Rocky hobbled out the door.

Sam was beginning to suspect that Franco's expertise wasn't an act. "You know, *you* ought to audition for the commercial."

"Bite your tongue. I would never stoop so low."

"I hear the residuals are pretty good."

"But once you appear in one, you are forever tainted."

"Judy Garland probably did commercials."

Sam knew immediately that she'd seriously erred.

Finger quivering, Franco pointed to the elevators. "Go!"

"Franco, I didn't mean to insult the goddess."

He turned his head away. "Be sure to wear the wrinkled beige to your presentation!"

"Franco, I apologized. And I do need your help."

"How you have the nerve to ask, I do not know."

"I have gos-sip," she said in a singsong voice.

Franco drew a deep breath and crossed his arms over his chest. "It would have to be gossip of the very highest caliber."

The words tumbled out of Sam's mouth. "Betty LaBrec arrived at the Carrington with full entourage and matching Louis Vuitton luggage. She carried a schnauzer with a Hermès dog collar."

"Color?"

"The schnauzer?"

"The *collar*."

"Orange."

Franco nodded, gesturing for her to continue and be snappy about it.

"Three bellmen, two carts and a chauffeur. White pantsuit. Turban. Sunglasses." Sam felt like she was running a race.

"Facelift," Franco murmured.

"When she discovered that, uh, Mrs. McGrath was not only in residence, but in Ms. LaBrec's usual suite, she threw a fit."

"Of course she did! Everyone knows they hate each other."

"Words were exchanged—"

"What words?"

"Angry words?" Darn. Why hadn't she asked? The gossip business was new to her. "Anyway, she made the grand exit claiming that she'll never set foot in the Carrington again. *And* she didn't tip.''

Nostrils bending inward, Franco inhaled deeply and held his breath. He and Sam stared at each other.

Franco exhaled. ''You are forgiven. And you wear the beige over my dead body. We will shop tomorrow for a suit in tomato-red. Red stimulates sales.''

Sam did a little exhaling herself. ''I'm leaving tomorrow.''

''We'll shop tonight.''

IT WAS ALMOST TOO EASY. Sam, in her tomato-red power suit, had given the FVA a bid they couldn't refuse. She felt so confident that she wore her suit on the plane home and hired a limo for the drive from the airport. A taxi just wasn't good enough. On the way into town, she toasted herself with a glass of champagne.

Knowing that FVA was all about families, Sam had proposed the Carrington Washington, D.C., and had created educational side trips to the Smithsonian and several different city tours. She'd managed entertainment to fit every budget. She'd created menus that were both kid friendly and appealed to adults. She'd practically given away the rooms. She'd guaranteed licensed baby-sitters. She'd even created a no-smoking, alcohol-free jazz club just for them. And, she'd pointed out the proximity to the government, in case they wanted to do a little lobbying.

No one else had ever offered them as much, she was certain. Yes, the convention would be labor-intensive, but the profit potential was enormous—and once those families became familiar with the Carrington Washington, D. C., they'd want to stay there when they returned. And maybe, just maybe, the board would vote to hold the convention there every year.

She'd left them stunned. Absolutely speechless. She could still see the look on their faces. Even now, they were probably kicking themselves for going with Josh all those years.

Sam held up her champagne glass and toasted her reflection in the smoked glass windows. Josh Crandall, eat your heart out.

When she arrived back at The Willoughby, she was amused to note that Franco had finally roused himself to act as doorman, probably to save face in front of the chauffeur.

Approaching the car, he whisked open the door. "Oh. It's just you."

"Hi, yourself." Sam swung her legs out and headed for the door, confident that her overnight case would follow.

After some pro forma muttering, Franco dumped the case at her feet when he reached the lobby. "So how did it go?"

Sam slung the strap over her arm. "I rule!" She punched the elevator button.

"I don't suppose there's any gossip in Tulsa."

Actually, Sam had scanned the *Tulsa Today* magazine while she was waiting for room service. "Just that Bill Duncan is appearing at the Windmill Dinner Theater."

Franco inhaled and made his nose move again, so Sam guessed the tidbit was better than she'd figured. She'd never heard of Bill Duncan.

"A dinner theater." Franco tsked, looking delighted. "How the mighty have fallen." He was on his cell phone before the elevator arrived.

SAM, A.J. AND CLAIRE HAD stayed up long past midnight talking and Sam was running late as she left the apartment the next morning. The others had already left for the day.

"Samaaantha?" Mrs. Higgenbotham stood in her doorway. Beside her, on a leash, was Cleo.

"Hi, Mrs. H." Sam locked the door. "I am *so* late!"

"Yes. Cleo has been waiting for her walksies."

A.J. and Claire had said something about walking Mrs. Higgenbotham's dog. Why, Sam didn't know. She wasn't a dog person. Or a cat person. Come to think of it, she was really more of a stuffed animal person. "Claire and A.J. have already left."

"Excellent. Now you and Cleo can get to know each other. I must tell you that Cleo feels you don't like her."

Smart dog. Sam looked into Cleo's accusing eyes.

"Her therapist was most insistent that I apprise you of the situation so that you could make amends."

Knowing it was fruitless to argue with a person whose dog was in therapy, Sam bent down and gingerly patted Cleo's apricot-tinted head. "Hi there, Cleo."

Cleo turned her head away.

How about that? There was a word for the way the dog was acting and in this situation, it was entirely appropriate.

"You see, Cleo? Samaaantha does not revile you."

Revile?

"You simply must go with her. I'm sure when you get back, you two will be the best of friends." Mrs. Higgenbotham handed Sam Cleo's leash.

"Sorry." Sam handed it back. "I'm on my way to work and I'm just swamped today." Sam made a mental note to buy Cleo a gourmet dog biscuit, if there was such a thing. Well, there had to be, if there were dog therapists. "Maybe some other time."

Mrs. Higgenbotham looked as though Sam had slapped her. "But it's time for Cleo's walksies!"

"Then you'll have to walk her." Sam didn't have time for this. People could only take advantage of you if you let them. Sam knew Mrs. Higgenbotham's type and it was important to be firm with them up front.

She started to walk past Mrs. Higgenbotham when the woman spoke.

"Marlon won't like to hear this."

Since Sam had to wait for the elevator anyway, she asked, "Who's Marlon?"

"He owns this building."

"And?" Sam didn't get the connection.

"Well, in the past, all Tavish's...guests have been so very *kind* to Cleo that I never got around to commenting on their extended stay and the fact that Tavish was never around when they were." She scooped up Cleo in a swirl of chiffon and closed the door.

It took a few seconds before Sam realized she and her roommates were being blackmailed. Walk Cleo and Mrs. Higgenbotham stays quiet about the sublet. Got it. What she didn't get was why Claire and A.J. had never told her about this shakedown. Maybe they liked the exercise.

Sam knocked on Mrs. Higgenbotham's door. When the woman opened it, Sam simply held out her hand.

"There, Cleo! You see?" Mrs. Higgenbotham kissed the dog, then set her down and handed Sam the leash—a leash of better quality leather than any of Sam's belts.

She smiled down at Cleo. *I'll get you, my pretty.* The dog looked back warily. Sam took off toward the elevator at the brisk pace she intended to set for the rest of the walk.

"Oh, good. Cleo does so love a run!"

Great. Just great.

AS IT TURNED OUT, THIS was not the day to be late getting to Carrington. Sam hadn't thought it would be so bad since she'd been traveling on company business and had returned after eight o'clock the night before. And she wasn't *that* late, since Cleo's brief run had inexplicably been cut short by the sight of a large, male poodle leading its owner, who didn't look as though she had a very firm grip on the leash.

The poodle had noticed Cleo immediately. If she had to guess, Sam would attribute it to the apricot tint. Except that dogs were color-blind, weren't they?

Sam slowed. "Hey, Cleo. Check out those pecs."

Cleo yelped and proceeded to tangle the leash in Sam's legs, then took off the way they came, ruining her pedicure as her nails scraped ineffectually on the sidewalk. "Cleo!"

As Cleo yelped hysterically, Sam bent down to try to

get some slack on the leash so she could step out of it when she heard a faint "Henri!" and felt hot poodle breath in an area it had no place being.

Straightening, Sam kicked off a shoe, freed her leg, grabbed the quivering Cleo, scraped her heel trying to get her shoe back on, and did a quick about-face. "Enough walksie for today!"

Still, it was well after nine—okay, nine-thirty—when Sam arrived at work. Tiffany pounced as soon as Sam entered the reception area. "Where have you been?"

"Tulsa." Sam refused to explain herself to a receptionist with delusions of importance.

"Mr. Hennesey's been looking for you. He wants to see you in the conference room."

Sam's heart picked up speed. This could be it. They could be announcing the new east coast manager. And she was late because of a psychotic poodle and her blackmailing owner. "Thanks, Tiffany."

Or maybe the Family Values Assembly board had called already! Though why they hadn't called her first—except she was just now getting into the office.

Since she was already late, Sam stopped by her cubicle to compose herself and check her hair and makeup, then headed for the conference room.

Conference room. That meant people. She wished Tiffany had given her a clue, but Tiffany rarely had a clue.

The door was closed. Sam hated, *hated* walking into conference rooms late and when the door was closed, she never knew if she should knock, and draw everyone's attention, or just walk in and take a seat.

She knocked. If she'd been planning to attend the

meeting, she wouldn't have, but all she was going on was Tiffany's message.

"Come in." It was Hennesey's voice. She thought.

Sam opened the door and was startled to find that the table was nearly full. A quick scan told her that the brass were all present and that the other candidates for the position weren't.

That was good, wasn't it?

And then she saw Josh. What was he doing here?

He met her eyes and for the first time she could remember, his ever-present smile was missing.

That could be good.

"Tiffany buzzed us that you were on your way," Hennesey said.

The ever-helpful Tiffany.

"Why don't you take that seat, Samantha?"

The end of the table. Not good. Nobody was smiling. Also not good.

Sam sat.

"We've had a call from the Family Values Assembly."

Well *that* was good. "Did they like my presentation?"

There was silence.

Sam's mind photographed the scene and seared it into her memory. Though only brief instants passed, she saw the way everyone avoided looking at her. Since when had pens become so fascinating? And the body language—stiff, turned away.

Except Josh. His smile, though subdued, was back and he had the same loose-limbed body language he always did, but his eyes—and he was the only one who'd meet her gaze—his eyes told her he was furious.

Ah. So that must mean the FVA had chosen Carrington. So why was everyone else acting liked she'd stepped in something?

"They didn't, ah, actually comment on your bid, Sam," Mr. Hennesey began, his tone measured. "Which I wish I'd known about in advance."

"I wanted to surprise you," she told him.

Josh winced.

Okay, that didn't come out right. "I felt it would be more efficient to bring the package to you all ready to be signed, sealed and delivered." Signed, sealed and delivered was one of Mr. Hennesey's pet sayings.

"There is no deal, Sam. FVA was extremely offended by your actions."

Offended? Sam blinked. *"What?* Why? It was a dream bid for them."

"That's what we're here to figure out."

What on earth could she possibly have done? "A copy of the bid package is on my desk."

Hennesey shook his head. "I'd like to see it, but it doesn't matter now. They claim they were badgered by a harridan of a woman."

Sam felt her jaw drop. "Me? They were talking about *me?* But I don't understand." She felt as though she'd walked into some else's nightmare.

At that, Hennesey gestured to Josh, who said, "That's where I come in."

SHE HAD NERVE, HE'D GIVE her that. Unexpected moxie. Too bad he was way too angry to appreciate it.

So she thought she could horn in on his territory, did she? Went on a rogue poaching expedition and probably would have succeeded, too, if she'd done as much research on *who* the FVA were as *what* they were.

Oh, she'd picked a good convention. It would have been a professional black eye for Josh if she'd snatched FVA away from Meckler even though Josh was no longer associated with them.

Fortunately for him, she hadn't succeeded. Even more fortunately for him, he was right here to learn all about it.

Poor Sam. He almost felt sorry for her. Almost.

It was time for a little personal damage control. "I do appreciate you trying to use some of my suggestions, Sam, but you clearly needed a little practice first."

"I didn't use any of your suggestions," she snapped.

"Maybe you should have," Hennesey shot back.

Josh could see her grit her teeth all the way from his position at the center of the table. "Your first mistake—or, I guess this would be your second, since not paying attention in class was your first mistake..." Josh was gratified to see that Sam was so hot he could probably fry an egg on her head. "Your *next* mistake was not opening the meeting with prayer."

"What the hell are you talking about?"

"Language like that would be another miscalculation. FVA is a faith-based organization. Leading them in a quick prayer would have reassured them that you were on their wavelength."

"Is that what you did?"

"Every time."

She didn't have to look so surprised. He knew his

way around the inside of a church. "I also quote liberally from the previous year's FVA opening keynote speech. They have them on their Web site."

"And they fell for it?"

Ooo, nice one. Josh spread his hands knowing that his record spoke for itself, but he was going to have to do something about Sam. He couldn't allow her to take these potshots at him.

She was looking at her boss. "I've found that people are very touchy about their religious preferences and it's best to avoid any mention of it."

"Avoiding is one thing," Josh said. "Showing up dressed like the devil is something else."

She inhaled sharply. "I did not!"

Mr. Hennesey rustled his notes. "They did mention a red outfit, Sam."

"Yes, I wore a new red suit. Red excites."

"Would have worked for me." Josh cleared his throat. "By that I mean your reasoning was sound, but this situation was the exception. FVA is a very conservative group. They don't want to be excited."

ALL RIGHT, ALL READY. Sam had blown it. She got the message. Now it was all about damage control—and not allowing Josh, of all people, to witness any more of her failure. "I understand that the Family Values Assembly has been offended in some way. But usually when clients get in a huff, they cancel. FVA isn't a client and hasn't been for years. We had nothing at stake. Other than wearing red and putting together the best package I've ever proposed to anyone, my conduct was the same as it always is."

Out of the corner of her eye she saw Josh shift and knew he was thinking about her one almost-lapse in professional judgment. He was letting her know it, too. Fine. She'd tried to embarrass him and failed. She expected him to rub it in. She could handle it.

"Normally, this would be considered nothing more than a failed bid. So why the big meeting?" Sam swept her arm in an arc indicating the Carrington bigwigs. Whatever they were going to do, she wanted them to get it over with. She'd taken a chance and failed. There were consequences. She accepted that.

Hennesey opened another file. From across the room, Sam could see some sort of computer-generated grid. "The FVA reaction, though extreme, isn't the first comment of its kind we've had during follow-up calls."

"No one has *ever*—"

Hennesey held up his hand. "I'm not saying I agree with them. You're an attractive young woman and some of the people you've approached aren't politically enlightened yet."

Oh, not the PC talk. Sam *hated* that kind of pussyfooting around.

"This meeting isn't to criticize you, Sam."

Up until now, it had sounded that way to *her*.

"In fact, I admire your initiative," Hennesey told her.

It was the first hope she'd had. Sam relaxed an infinitesimal amount.

"But," Mr. Hennesey continued, "you're being considered for a top-level position and we need to address this issue. People think you come on too strong."

Sam's mother had warned her about this. Repeatedly. Sam's sisters had told her of their experiences and still, Sam couldn't believe that in this day and age, she was hearing such talk.

"All is not lost," Josh spoke. "My research has shown that the problem of abrasive women is more common than we realize. I've got to give FVA points for being open about it. Most groups wouldn't have admitted it."

Sam didn't want to give FVA any points.

And she didn't want to give Josh any, either.

"You see," Josh said, settling in his chair, "women have had to fight to be taken seriously for so long that some of them have overcompensated. They need to learn how to soften their approach and use their other strengths."

If that wasn't an oxymoron, Sam didn't know what was.

"I recommend that Sam attend the Fiery Femmes corporate coaching. They've done some good work in retraining women executives who..." He looked at her consideringly. "Who intimidate in their interpersonal relations."

"People are intimidated because they're incompetent. That's not my problem."

"Well, Sam, according to what your boss just said, it *is* your problem." Lucky for him, Josh's tone stopped just short of being patronizing.

"We want Sam to learn to be less abrasive," Mr. Hennesey said. "This 'Fiery Femmes' sounds like the opposite of what we're trying to achieve. She's already fiery enough."

"It's marketing," Josh said. "No one would go to something called Wimpy Women. Now, they've got a three-month, weekly—"

"Three months!" He was crazy. They were all crazy.

"And a two-week immersion retreat." Josh looked at her. "You'd have to stay on their site."

This was nightmare city. In two weeks, Leonard and Harvey—more likely Harvey—could solidify their position while Sam...

While Sam had no choice. This was the price of failure. She might as well get on with it.

Josh was looking very self-satisfied.

He could gloat for now, but Sam resolved to turn this to her advantage. Somehow. "Okay. Two weeks it is. When do I start?"

7

"YOU WANT TO SUE? I would *love* to represent you."

A.J. and Claire sat on Sam's bed in roommately solidarity while Sam packed for her two-week sojourn.

"This attitude is archaic," Claire said. "And I should know."

"No lawsuit. I'm going to take my medicine." Sam held up two tops. She was having a hard time choosing between her old wardrobe and her new color-enhanced pieces.

Both A.J. and Claire pointed to the China-blue shell. Sam tossed it over a chair and hung the other top back up. "This is Josh's revenge and he's entitled."

"How can you say that?" Claire asked.

"I attacked his turf. I lost. This is his way of getting back at me."

"And there is always the tiniest, minuscule possibility that he could be right about you being too aggressive."

"Claire!" Both Sam and A.J. protested.

"All I'm saying is that you—and you, too, A.J.—have a take-no-prisoners style that can be a little, well, you know." She seemed to shrink under the combined glares of A.J. and Sam.

"Attack someone else before your own incompetence is revealed. Oldest trick in the book," A.J. said.

"That's what these whiners are doing. I wish Sam hadn't given in."

"By doing so, I ended the meeting. It was an inevitable outcome, so I cut short the look-what-Sam-did-wrong phase." She tossed in the wrinkled beige suit Franco hated. At least it was nonthreatening. The brochure had said there was going to be a wardrobe analysis.

"Good strategy," A.J. said.

"Well, guys, what else should I pack?"

"How about something pink?" Claire suggested.

"Pink?" Sam made a gagging gesture. "That wasn't one of my colors *before* I knew what my colors were."

A.J. made an X with her fingers.

"You two." Claire slid off the bed and went to her room. "I've got a sweater..."

Sam dumped underwear into the suitcase. Her underwear was serviceable and comfortable and she was drawing the line there. Well, almost there. For some reason, she tossed in a set of dating underwear when A.J. was distracted by Claire's return.

"Try this." Claire held up a pink fuzzy sweater that screamed "girl." "Men love this sweater."

"But Claire..." Sam looked at her tiny roommate. "It probably won't fit me."

"So it's a little tight. All the better. Are there going to be any men there?"

"I don't know."

"If they're going to coach you to not threaten men, it's logical that at some point you'll have to interact with them."

"I like the way she thinks," A.J. said.

Sam took the sweater and held it against her. The soft pink truly wasn't her color, but did she look that awful in it? She looked...cuddly in a high school kind of way.

"Take the skirt, too," Claire suggested. "You'll be invincible."

OH, WHAT A WONDERFUL day's work. Each time Josh thought about that meeting, he could see Sam's face. Her expression when he told Hennesey all about Fiery Femmes...priceless. And just wait until she got there... He grinned.

Sam had this coming to her. That would teach her to go after his clients. Technically former clients, but everyone knew Family Values was Josh's. That she dared try to steal it away meant she was seriously ticked at him over the training sessions and his suggestions that she modify her approach.

Actually, the idea behind Fiery Femmes was solid, even though it had hard-core feminists up in arms. He could see their point, but it came down to what a person was willing to do to succeed. Josh, personally, was willing to do quite a lot and he figured Sam was, too.

They were exactly alike in that way.

He wished they weren't so much alike.

He wished—

A knock announcing his next individual coaching session sounded on the conference room door. Josh strode across the room, but he paused, hand on the knob and allowed himself exactly three seconds to relive the feel of Sam in his arms, the warmth of her mouth, the way her hand traced the edge of his ear before she buried her fingers in his hair and held him to her.

Yeah, he could remember a lot in three seconds.

And then he pushed the memories away and opened the door.

"WELCOME TO FIERY FEMMES, where we put out the flames without dousing the fire. I'm Grace Halston."

Sam sighed. Was she doomed to two weeks of slogans? She checked out the other eighteen women in the room and not one of them looked happy to be here.

None of these women would have whined about Sam being too aggressive. These were Sam's kind of women. She wished her mother were here to see this—not the whole FF concept, but these women who were all at the upper echelons of their companies. A lot more upper than Sam, as a matter of fact. Sam thought she might be one of the youngest, if not *the* youngest, but these days, with dermabrasion, botox and facelifts, a person couldn't tell by looking.

"Your companies have sent you here not because you need help in doing your jobs, but because the way you interact with co-workers has made you less effective."

Yeah, yeah. Tell it to the sales figures.

"You are, in a word, frightening."

No, *this* was frightening.

But not as frightening as seeing the person escorted by two FF personnel who appeared in the doorway. Sam stared, certain that she was hallucinating. It surely wasn't...it couldn't be... It was. Of course it was. Why wouldn't it be? Why wouldn't the person she wanted *least* to see be standing in the doorway grinning his you-gotta-like-me grin?

"Hello, Mr. Crandall. We're just getting started. Why don't you sit in the seat over here?" Ms. Halston—at least she allowed Ms.—stepped to the side and indicated one of the chairs in the second of two rows.

Sam had a couple of problems with that, problems other than Josh's presence. First, the language. "Why don't you..." Typical feminine speech patterns that she constantly attempted to eliminate in her own speech. Also, Ms. Halston was the director of Fiery Femmes, yet she was acting like a hostess. Josh was an uncouth lout who was late, yet they all had to wait while he came in and was catered to by the highest-ranking female.

And, yes, what *was* he doing here?

She hoped he was enjoying himself. Spectacular as his revenge was, this was a long drive just to gloat. The Fiery Femmes campsite was hidden away in the Adirondacks, probably to discourage escape.

And it was indeed a campsite. It was on the rough-hewn side, which Sam hadn't expected from the plush bus that had discreetly ferried her and her fiery sisters from Manhattan. Really, she appreciated nature as much as the next person—from a distance—but what did roughing it have to do with becoming more feminine? Roughing it was very unfeminine.

And what was with the roommate? For what Carrington was paying, Sam had expected a junior suite at the least.

When she'd first seen the lodge house, Sam had visions of long hikes followed by a massage and some hot tub time.

Ha.

She shifted on the folding chair and tuned back into Ms. Halston.

"I, myself, was once a fiery femme. In fact, I was a fired femme." There was polite laughter. Ms. Halston, Grace as she wanted to be called, continued with the usual meant-to-be-inspirational stories of her struggle and how she decided to start Fiery Femmes to save other women from suffering as she did...blah blah blah.

Sam slid a glance toward Josh and found him with a pious look on his face as he listened, head tilted to show that he agreed with the speaker. Sam knew all his tricks now.

Ms. Halston, Grace, was telling about the grounds and the routine. "Although that isn't the main reason we're here, many of our clients find that they lose weight..."

Okay. Could be good. Sam wouldn't mind losing a couple of pounds. Maybe more, so she could have all the fun of putting them back on.

Sam relaxed and let her mind wander. Actually, if she looked on this as a vacation...took in a little hiking...

"...introduce Josh Crandall, founder of Perfect Pitch Seminars..." No. No. A thousand times no. "...who has graciously agreed to discuss body language with us." Grace stood back and applauded.

Not again. Not only had Sam heard this lecture before, she knew, just *knew* that Josh would use her as an example. *That* was why he was here. Just having Sam sent to Fiery Femmes wasn't enough. He'd come all this way to humiliate her, too.

And she'd actually kissed him once. Twice. Okay, several times, but only on the one occasion and never, never, never would again.

Never.

"Normally, we wouldn't plunge right in with the lectures, but we're at the mercy of Mr. Crandall's schedule."

"Call me Josh." He ambled to the front and swept the room with a smile. With one exception, the female audience perked up.

Oh, please. Couldn't they tell that he'd probably spent half an hour fooling with his hair so that it had that I-just-ran-my-fingers-through-it look? And the way he drew his hands to his hips so his unbuttoned jacket was pushed aside to reveal his flat stomach. Ducking his head slightly...the grin...Sam had seen it all before. She was immune.

As Josh began his patter, she stared out the window at the late afternoon sun filtering through the trees in golden beams. It really was pretty here. And peaceful. She should concentrate on that instead of her rapidly rising blood pressure. She'd never had high blood pressure, but she did now.

"Unfortunately, my lovely assistant couldn't accompany me, so I'll need someone to help me with the demonstrations."

Here it was, and so soon. Sam braced herself for further humiliation.

He stepped forward. "How about you?"

Sam dragged her gaze from the window and prepared to stand.

But a woman seated three seats down from her stood and walked to the front. A blond woman. A blond woman with long, golden legs wearing white denim shorts.

Well, good. She'd keep him distracted.

And she did. Maybe a little *too* distracted. In fact, Josh and Julia—didn't that sound cute together?—were having a grand old time. Julia, didn't seem all that swift, since Josh had to keep touching her to position her arms, shoulders and face. Couldn't he just tell her to move them where he wanted them for heaven's sake?

For a high-powered, intimidating woman, Julia sure giggled a lot.

And Sam couldn't help noticing how a blonde really set off Josh's dark good looks.

Stop it.

If she didn't know better, Sam would swear she was jealous. Right. She was *so* not jealous. He could ask Julia to dinner right in front of everyone and Sam wouldn't care. He could even *kiss* her and Sam wouldn't care. At least not much, and only because it would remind her of the time Josh had kissed *her*—not that kissing Josh was all that great, now that she thought about it—so Julia was welcome to all of Josh's insincere kisses she wanted.

Not that she would want many, because Julia was no doubt smarter than Sam had been and would be able to tell that Josh was all style and no substance right away, whereas it had taken Sam several kisses of various lengths and depths.

Julia tossed her blond hair—like that was so intimidating—and let Josh loom over her—no doubt he was checking out her suprasternal notch—as he uncrossed her arms and positioned her hands palms downward.

What was Julia doing here, anyway? She couldn't intimidate a puppy. Witness Josh's unintimidated puppy dog eyes.

Speaking of, he hadn't looked at Sam *at all* to see if she was demonstrating his stupid positions of negation correctly. In fact, she had a position of negation she'd like to demonstrate to him privately.

During the entire lecture and demonstration, Grace fluttered about giving everyone encouragement. Was this the way they were all supposed to act at the end of the course? Personally, Sam was not about to turn herself into a damn butterfly in order to get a promotion.

At last, Josh's lecture was over. After exchanging cards with everyone—again with one exception—he was escorted out. Just before he walked out of sight, he caught Sam's eyes and gave her a quick two-fingered salute.

She wanted to respond with a one-finger salute, but didn't dare. His grin told her he knew exactly what she was thinking.

Good riddance.

But as soon as Josh was out of sight, an extraordinary thing happened. Fluttery Grace transformed into Ms. Halston, the Ms. Halston who had once been a fiery femme. She dropped all softness and took on a no-nonsense attitude.

"The first thing on our agenda will be to divide into teams so we can assign chores."

Wait a minute. Chores? Nobody said anything about chores. There had been no talk of chores in front of *Josh*.

Ms. Halston—nobody wanted to call her Grace any-more—continued with a brief overview of the program. Sam listened closely and discovered that yes, each "camper" was expected to do chores. They had to be kidding. Had she gotten on the bus to the Betty Ford Clinic by mistake? And the daily schedule...where was the downtime? What if she didn't *want* to hike at 5:00 a.m.?

She knew what this was. This was one of those break-your-spirit places so they could all be brain-washed easier.

"You actually expect us to clean and cook?" some-one asked.

"If you want to eat," Ms. Halston returned serenely. She'd obviously heard that one before. "You must learn to work together as a team."

"Why?"

"To bond."

"Again, why?"

Sam wasn't going to say a word. This wasn't the time to question the program. This was the time to do as they were told so they could go back to their compa-nies and pretend to be all meek and mild so real meek and mild people who had managed to work their way into a position of influence—no doubt because they were related to, or sleeping with, the boss—could pretend they were truly powerful.

But Ms. Halston didn't seem annoyed. "You need to bond because as the week progresses, you will have to give each other feedback which will be more accurate if you know each other and your working styles. Which brings us to our most important tenet—no visitors and no phone calls."

The room erupted at that. Ms. Halston waited impassively for the worst of it to blow over, then held up her hands, palms outward. "Your careers depend on what you learn here. There is much to absorb in the next two weeks and you will have to concentrate. You do not need the distractions of visitors or phone calls to the office. The world can function without you. And no, there is no Internet connection here. After orientation, you will have one hour to contact those you feel you need to. After that, I will ask that you surrender your cell phones."

There was more, but Sam just let it wash over her. *Resistance is futile.* She smiled wearily to herself. Someday, she'd get Josh back for this. It was just that there was so much to get him back for.

A WEEK HAD PASSED AND Josh knew he should feel guilty at the thought of Sam stuck in that place, but he didn't. In fact, she should be thanking him. For one thing, the Fiery Femmes center looked like one of those ritzy spas—the faux rough kind. The grounds were immaculate and the rooms they'd shown him, as well as the public areas, were clean and well-kept. The menu looked great. The place must have an excellent maintenance crew.

They probably kept a masseuse on staff, too. Josh hunched his shoulders and rolled them forward. He could use a massage.

He could use a break, period. He was tired of analyzing videos of sweaty salesmen trying to sell him on their hotels and hotel managers learning how to deal with irate patrons.

Yeah, a break was sounding good. He needed to get out of the city. Maybe a drive into upstate New York, say, toward the Adirondacks....

WEEK ONE HAD ENDED. Sam had survived. Actually, the whole thing had taken on a Girl Scout camp atmosphere and since one of the team members was a chef who couldn't keep a kitchen staff, the food was pretty good.

Sam, who'd drawn kitchen duty, was packing lunches. Today shouldn't be very bad, either. There was a mock meeting drill scheduled which did have some potential amusement value. Each of them was assigned a certain personality for the meeting and charged with acting in character for the person running the meeting.

They were always playacting. There was the termination drill, the job interview, and the most fun so far, the job assessment.

Marty, a gruff woman from Philadelphia, had founded her own business and resented that her family had sent her to Fiery Femmes. "No, I'm not giving you a raise," she said in her assessment interview. "You're incompetent, that's why. You should be glad I'm not firing you. And since I own the company, I could, government be damned."

There was spontaneous applause and then Grace Halston made them write a more empathetic script. "I hear that you are having personal issues..."

If Sam had to say "I hear" or "I understand" one more time, she'd throw up.

But at least the afternoon session was outside, hence the picnic lunches. Since Sam wasn't in the hot seat today, she figured she might even enjoy herself.

"I'M SORRY, MR. CRANDALL. Participants aren't allowed to have visitors."

Josh tried his smile on the receptionist. It didn't work. "Don't you remember me? I was here last week."

She nodded.

"I was sort of a visiting professor."

She didn't nod this time.

"Well, okay, can I come take a look around if I promise not to bother Ms. Baldwin?"

"No. We have a strict no-visitors policy."

Josh rested his arms on the file cabinet beside the receptionist and leaned forward. "Aw, I'm not just a visitor. I'm more like a—a super visitor."

"We don't allow super visitors, either."

The woman had no sense of humor. He thought about flirting with her, then asking her to take off her glasses and let down her hair, except that she wasn't wearing glasses and her hair was in a short shaggy cut.

"Can you at least do something for me. I've been trying to call her on her cell, but it must not be in range here. I'd like you to give her a message..." He trailed off as the receptionist shook her head.

"Participants don't have access to their phones. We only allow emergency phone calls."

Josh was dumbfounded, but resolved not to show it. "Aw, c'mon. This is an emergency."

"You'll have to come back next week." She didn't even ask him the nature of his emergency.

Josh didn't think appealing to her romantic side would work either. Anyway, as soon as Sam saw him, the romance cover would be blown.

"Then I'll see you next week when the session ends," he said lightly and went back to the car.

He'd driven way too far to leave without seeing Sam, rules or no rules. Nothing in the literature he'd seen mentioned this policy, other than a paragraph describing the remote location and lack of distractions.

Josh started the car and drove around the perimeter of the property, looking for a hole in the fence or another way in.

He didn't have a plan; he'd just started driving. And as he drove, he noticed the height of the fence for the first time. And the sharp razor wire across the top.

Was that to keep the prisoners—participants—in, or bad guys out?

If the receptionist had let him in, Josh would have looked around, razzed Sam a bit, and left. Now, it was a challenge, a quest, and hey, he was already stuck in the middle of New York State with nothing to do.

When Josh ran out of pavement, he parked the car, got out and walked. And walked. He wasn't dressed for a woodlands hike, but still he kept going and was finally rewarded when he heard the sound of voices. Female voices, and a lot of them.

Josh followed the fence through the trees and came upon them all at once. He froze because if he could see them, they could see him. But they weren't looking at him. Everyone was sitting on the ground watching two women cry.

He saw Sam right away. She sat, holding her knees to her chest. She wore jeans and a T-shirt. It was the first time he'd seen her dressed so casually and, well, she looked un-Sam-like. He liked it.

Maybe a little too much. He hadn't seen her in a week, so he allowed himself to look at her for a few moments, trying to appreciate her as a woman, just a woman. Not Sam. Just an attractive woman sitting on the ground on a summer afternoon in the woods with her hair caught up in one of those clip things that let a few bits dangle down the back of her neck. But it *was* Sam and that was the problem. He couldn't have an intimate relationship with Sam. It wouldn't work and trying to have one would destroy the relationship they had, dysfunctional though it was. Of course, after this, she'd probably never speak to him again, but at least she'd be a better saleswoman.

Just then something must have happened because all

the women stood and huddled. No, it was a group hug. Stupid touchie-feelie stuff.

Josh used the distraction to back away until he was more concealed. Then he sat on the matted grass and decomposing leaves left from last fall and watched.

Grace Halston, the woman Josh knew was in charge, spoke, "Is there anyone here who didn't feel sympathy for Naomi?"

Though there was a lot of looking at each other, no one raised her hand.

"Vulnerability can be a strength. Do not be afraid to cry or stammer or admit that you're hurt. It's much more effective than screaming at people or going all stiff and saying nothing."

What?

"Let's prepare for scenario number three. Nancy is presenting, Julia is the superior..."

Josh watched them role-play. He watched for way longer than he'd intended to. Frankly, he didn't like what he saw.

Sure, he knew that Fiery Femmes taught women to be less aggressive, but he hadn't expected them to become snivelly whiners.

And he really didn't like the way they were taught passive body language. It was completely opposite from his own theories. So therefore, it was wrong.

He shifted, the seat of his pants uncomfortably damp. He was thirsty, too, and had watched as the women had taken a break. But he'd remained and was treated to round two of "How to Lose Power in Meetings." It wasn't a pretty sight.

There were ways for women like Sam to be coached to become less abrasive yet still remain assertive. This wasn't it. And he'd gone on record recommending the Fiery Femmes program to other executive women.

Not good.

"...break for the afternoon. Remember that today, we rotate chores. Kitchen will go to grounds detail, grounds will rotate to lavatories, lavatories move to vacuuming and vacuumers will be our cooks."

Chores? Josh was stunned. He'd had no idea. From what he'd seen and learned, he didn't want his company to be associated with Fiery Femmes. He didn't want any of his recommendations appearing on their literature and he certainly didn't want their name on his.

Literature. He winced as he realized he'd have to re-print several thousand brochures. So much for buying in bulk.

But even worse, these people had Sam in their clutches. A little petty revenge was one thing, but this was entirely different. Harvey Wannerstein had been skulking around doing who knew what, but the person really concerning Josh was Leonard Sheffield. With Sam gone, he'd blossomed and had become a threat to her. Josh had done what he could to counter Leonard's maneuverings, but the man, perhaps because of his fishlike personality, had proved very slippery.

Josh continued to sit there after the women left. He'd messed up. Really messed up. And Sam was the one who was going to be affected. She must really hate him now and he couldn't blame her. And if she didn't hate him now, she would when she got back and found that she'd lost ground in the promotion race.

Josh didn't want her hating him—not the real kind. Disliking was fine—safe, even, but hating...hating was what he was trying to avoid.

Eventually, Josh stood and brushed off the back of his pants, then headed to his car. He was going to have to make this right.

Once he got to his car, he drove to the nearest village and bought two bottles of water and a pair of wire cutters.

8

IT WAS WARDROBE CHECK night and Sam, wearing Claire's fuzzy pink sweater and the skirt, stood in front of a panel of three drooling men.

Grace Halston frowned. "Yes, Sam, you do look non-threatening—"

"She looks great. I give her a thumbs-up," said one man.

"Definitely. No one could object to that," another man said.

"Ditto," the third man chimed in. "And I might add that her outfit is the best we've seen tonight."

The three men barely blinked as they stared at her.

Not to take anything away from Claire's sweater, but the skirt was really something. Until now, Sam thought Tavish's reaction when they rented the apartment was a fluke, but these men would probably have signed away their life insurance policies if she'd asked. Maybe she should.

Behind her, irritated whispers rustled. Sam could guess what her fellow femmes were saying. Her outfit—okay, maybe the sweater was a *little* tight—didn't look like anything special. None of the women had thought anything of it until they'd seen the men's reaction. Even Grace Halston couldn't figure it out.

But Sam knew it had to be the skirt. That was the

only explanation. And the Fiery Femmes women didn't like the way the men were ignoring them. Sam, herself, didn't understand the appeal, but she wasn't going to argue with results.

"Nevertheless, Samantha, will you please change into a suit so we can evaluate it?"

"Sure." Sam gleefully returned to her room. She would simply add a jacket and continue to wear the skirt. She had this wardrobe thing nailed.

She unlocked the door, walked into the room and stopped, staring at two suitcases on her bed. Her suitcases. And they had clothes in them. What was going on? She took a couple of steps forward and heard a sound.

A sound very much like someone else was in the room.

Her entire life's supply of adrenaline shot into her bloodstream. She inhaled to scream when a hand clamped across her mouth.

Sam immediately jabbed an adrenaline-powered elbow into her assailant's midsection then kicked backward for all she was worth.

She was apparently worth a lot because the force of her kick propelled them backward onto her roommate's bed. What followed was a lot of viciously whispered swearing during which she heard her name.

Sam stopped struggling, now aware that she was lying on top of Josh. Why he was in her room, she'd explore later. She stared at the ceiling and drew several deep breaths, trying to slow her heart rate. Trying not to be aware of Josh beneath her. Or his heart beating against her back. Or the way the skirt had gone all molten and warm. Kinda like some other parts of her body.

Her heart wasn't slowing. If anything, the rapid, shallow beats of a minute ago had turned into heavy thumps. She felt Josh's arms move and anticipated not only his caress, but her reaction to it, a reaction that would in no way hinder his progress as his hands skimmed her skirt-clad thighs, curved over her stomach and traveled toward—

"I can't breathe," Josh said.

Or caress, he might have added. "Well, I can't move." Her muscles were quivering.

"Try. Try very hard."

Moaning, Sam rolled off him, dragging the skirt with her. Inhaling, Josh drew up his leg and rubbed his shin.

"You scared me!" Sam said into the bedspread.

"Yeah, I kind of figured that."

"What were you thinking?"

"I didn't know if you were alone, or not."

"It's a good thing I was." She moved her head until she could see him. "What are you doing here?"

"Right now, I'm attempting to suppress any unmanly moaning."

"And then what?"

He turned his head and looked at her. He had long eyelashes. Sam had never noticed Josh's eyelashes before, not that there was any reason she should have. Or should now, for that matter, having failed with the whole caressing thing.

The corner of his mouth quirked upward. "I'm here to rescue you. Surprise."

"Rescue me from what?"

"From the antifeminist brainwashers."

"What are you talking about?"

"This place. They've got you held prisoner here."

"Yes, but that's so we can concentrate without out-side distractions."

He moaned. "It's started. Now I'll have to depro-gram you."

Sam chuckled and raised herself on an elbow, pleased when it didn't collapse. "Seriously, what are you doing here, and by here, I mean in this room ap-parently packing my things?"

Their gazes connected in one of those moments of awareness. Sam didn't want to be having any more awareness with or of Josh. She didn't want to notice that for once, his expression was open and unguarded. She didn't want to notice his eyes scanning her face or the fact that he liked what he saw. They'd been down that road before. But the thing Sam didn't want to no-tice most of all was that she wouldn't mind traveling down the road again, if they could turn right instead of left when they approached a certain intersection.

His voice was gruff when he spoke. "Seriously, I'm here to get you out of this place."

"But I'm supposed to stay another week. We're in the middle of wardrobe check. And Josh, it's night."

He heaved himself to his side and gingerly mas-saged his midsection. "Of course it's night. This is a breakout. Don't you know anything about escaping?"

"No."

"Trust me. This is the way it's done."

"Josh, I appreciate the thought—or do I? Anyway, thanks, but no thanks."

"Mmm-mmm-mmm." Wincing, he got up and limped over to the bathroom. "I couldn't tell which of this junk in here is yours."

"You don't need to know." Sam pushed herself off the bed and straightened the spread.

"Then you pack it." Avoiding her eyes, he came out of the bathroom and went to the dresser.

"I'm not going to pack because I'm not going with you."

"Yes, you are."

"I don't get it. You're the one who got me sent here."

"And now I'm the one springing you." He opened a drawer, looked at Sam's underwear, then shut it and opened another drawer containing her roommate's lacy, filmy, thongy underthings. Nodding to himself he scooped them up and dumped the armful in one of the suitcases.

Sam sighed. "Uh, Josh?"

"Hmm?" He finally looked up at her.

She shook her head.

"You mean..." He gestured to the underwear in the suitcase.

"No."

Hooking a thumb over his shoulder at the dresser. "Not..."

Sam nodded her head "yes."

"Oh." His face was a combination of disappointment and disapproval as he gathered Sam's roommate's underwear and stuffed it back in the drawer.

She just so happened to be wearing her turquoise date underwear—well, they'd been *told* to dress feminine—but she wasn't going to tell him. "Not like that. You've got to fold it."

He grabbed Sam's underwear and tossed it at the suitcase. "We don't have time."

"I'll make time. I mean, what is my roommate going to think when she finds her undies like that?"

"Do you care?" Josh checked the other drawers.

"Yes! And leave my stuff alone. I'm not going with you."

"Oh, you're going with me if I have to conk you on the head and toss you over my shoulder." He looked determined and manly and strong and in charge.

Sam didn't know what to think.

Actually, she kind of liked it.

Until Josh dumped her shoes on top of her underwear. "Hey!"

He gave her a stern look. "I've gone to a lot of trouble. Some might even say breaking—cutting actually—and entering. Now it's time for exiting and you're coming with me. I close the suitcases in sixty seconds. Whatever isn't in them gets left behind."

She'd argue later. Sam pushed her way past him to the bathroom and dumped all her makeup into her cosmetics bag, hoping the lids were on tight.

Josh was being a little too me-man-you-woman and she was liking it a little too much.

No one had ever rescued her before. Come to think of it, she hadn't needed rescuing before, not until Josh's little revenge. There's a point she shouldn't forget.

When she came out of the bathroom, hair dryer cord dragging on the ground, he'd already zipped up one of the suitcases.

"Josh?"

He turned around and then an extraordinary thing happened. He stared at her, which wasn't all that extraordinary, but the expression on his face was. It was as though he'd been hit in the head and was now seeing her in an entirely different way.

Sam knew that look. She'd just seen that look on three male Fiery Femme consultants. She'd seen that look on her landlord's face and now she was seeing it on Josh's.

Oh, ho. The skirt was working its magic. Sam could feel it rippling against her and when she looked down, it glowed with a rich, lustrous sheen.

She looked back up at Josh, but he'd turned away and was fitting her shoes around the edges of the suitcase. That's not the way it was supposed to work. At this point, he should be salivating, unable to drag his eyes away. He should be a zombie, ready to do her bidding.

At the thought, Sam experienced a wholly unexpected, but very enjoyable thrill.

"I don't think there's room in this suitcase for that bag," Josh said.

"Then we'll put it in the other one." Sam hoped he'd turn back around. She wanted to see if the skirt affected him the way it seemed to affect other men.

But he wouldn't look at her. He held out his hand behind him. Sam, knowing she was playing a dangerous game, sauntered toward him until she was practically touching him and handed him her cosmetics bag and hair dryer.

Josh snatched them from her, crammed them in an

outer pocket of the suitcase and zipped it closed. "We're outta here."

So much for proximity.

Without looking back at her—or pulling out the handles so he could wheel the luggage—he grabbed both suitcases and took off.

Sam hesitated. When her roommate saw her underwear drawer, she'd think Sam was some kind of pervert. Or a thief. But when her roommate realized nothing was missing that would eliminate the thief part, which left the pervert part.

Sam heard Josh's voice outside the door. "We can do this with you conscious or unconscious."

Speaking of perverts...Sam grabbed her satchel and quickly followed him.

Josh had propped open one of the exits. And no alarm had gone off? Great security.

"This way." Josh walked toward the woods away from the front drive and parking lot.

"Where are you going?"

"To my car, unless you prefer walking all the way back to New York."

"I prefer to stay here."

"No, you don't."

No, she didn't. "Don't tell me what I want."

"You let *them* tell you what you want."

"That was the whole idea!"

"It...it was a bad idea."

The entire conversation so far had taken place with Sam talking to the back of Josh's head. The more she hurried to catch up with him, the faster he walked. She was practically jogging now. "Stop."

"Keep walking. I don't want to get caught."

"Josh, I'm wearing heels!"

He stopped until she caught up, but didn't look back. "Sorry."

"And what do you think will happen if they *do* catch us? This isn't a prison, it's an executive training retreat. No one has broken any laws. Except, maybe, you."

"Oh, definitely me." He exhaled and set her suitcases down. Still avoiding looking at her, he drew his hands to his waist and stared into the distance. "I've, uh, never done anything like this before."

"What happened to Mr. Trust-me-this-is-how-it's-done?"

"The escaping part is intuitive. I meant..." He gestured.

"Meant what?"

"The...changing my mind part."

"What do you mean?" Sam stepped around until she was facing him. He looked so...so un-Josh-like. She got another one of those I'm-looking-at-an-attractive-man zings.

It occurred to her that her relationship with Josh—such that it was—was full of zings of one kind or another. And it also occurred to her to wonder just how many zings a body could stand without some unzinging.

Josh stared everywhere but at her. "I saw your session this afternoon. And later, I saw you working outside. I heard them talking about chores—"

"It wasn't so bad. Chores are so we'll bond."

"This isn't rehab."

"In a way it is. We have to abandon old behaviors and learn new ones."

He picked up her suitcases and started walking again. "I didn't like it."

"Neither did I, but my promotion was on the line. Maybe even my job. Something I'm doing is offending our clients. I can't continue—"

"Sam, you're fine."

Sure, *now* she's fine. "That's not what you said to Mr. Hennesey."

He walked faster. "I had no business telling Hennesey anything."

"But—"

"I changed my mind, okay? Can we just drop it?"

Sam didn't want to drop anything, but Josh was acting so weird she decided to bring it up again later.

They tramped along toward the back of the property in silence until Josh set her suitcases down next to the chain-link fence.

"There's a hole," Sam pointed out. "A nice-sized one, too. And look, the edges are folded back. How did you ever find such a convenient hole, Josh?"

"Just climb through," he said wearily.

Sam stared at the hole in the fence. This made it real. She actually was escaping from Fiery Femmes in the dead of night. Okay, it was only about nine o'clock, but close enough.

It appeared that Josh had gone to no little effort on her behalf. The question was why? Sam believed she'd already asked that and had yet to receive a satisfactory answer.

"Please?"

Wow. His voice was more ragged than the edges of the fence. Sam climbed through. Josh pushed her luggage after her, then climbed through, himself.

"Hang on a minute." Reaching into his pocket, Josh withdrew wire cutters and snipped the tie-wraps holding the fence apart. Carefully, he bent the fence back into place, then secured the edges with more of the plastic wraps.

"And you wouldn't let me refold my roommate's underwear."

Josh glanced at her before picking up her suitcases. "I wouldn't want some animal to get in there and hurt anyone," he mumbled. "The car's this way."

"I see it." Sam walked ahead this time.

Josh's car was a rental, a sedate black import. He blipped the alarm. So much for a stylish escape. Sam put her satchel in the back seat while he stowed her suitcases in the trunk.

The strained silence continued as they got into the car. Or maybe it wasn't strained to Josh, but Sam was still unclear on what exactly had led them to the point where she had climbed through a fence to get away from a very expensive training seminar.

She remained quiet until Josh made it back to the two-lane highway. "I'm going to assume that Hennesey doesn't know about this."

Josh hesitated. "No."

"Great." She looked over at him. His face was grim. "What am I supposed to tell him? Leaving halfway through is bound to affect my chances for the promotion."

"I'll think of something."

"And, though we aren't particularly close, my room-mate is going to say something when I don't respond to bed check."

"They actually checked to see if you were there each night?" Josh glanced over at her and just as quickly dragged his gaze away.

"I was being rhetorical."

He exhaled. "They—they...I didn't—what I mean is, um...Fiery Femmes is on the right track, but they derailed somewhere."

How about that? Mr. Self Confidence was stammering. And since when did a stammering man give her a zing?

"I, uh, should have picked up on that," he mumbled.

Was Josh trying to apologize? The evening was getting better and better.

"And—and I'll make it right with Hennesey."

"No. I should do that."

"I don't mind," he said quickly.

"I do. I don't want to look as though I can't handle sticky situations."

"But you wouldn't be *in* this sticky situation if I hadn't recommended that you go to Fiery Femmes."

"I wouldn't be in this sticky situation if you hadn't broken me out of Fiery Femmes. And don't think I won't mention that."

Josh gripped the steering wheel.

"I won't make you look too bad." Sam was enjoying his discomfiture.

"Don't worry about me. Worry about Leonard Sheffield."

Wait a minute... "What about him?"

"He's morphed into an actual contender. I think I've contained him, though."

The thought of Josh "containing" Leonard for her struck Sam as funny. In fact, now that they were in the car, the whole situation was funny. But Josh was so seriously contrite that Sam wanted to milk it. She turned toward the window and smothered a laugh.

"Sam?"

At the guilt in his voice, she nearly snorted. This was great. This was really great.

"Sam, I am *so* sorry." The words poured out of Josh. "I had no idea that place was so bad. You've got to believe me. Yeah, I was mad that you went after Family Values, but I would never have done anything that would have...oh, hell, Sam, don't cry."

He thought she was *crying.* She wasn't a crier and was about to tell him so when he continued.

"I am scum—"

"A scummy jerk."

"Yeah, I know it and I *will* make this up to you."

Fiery Femmes had promoted crying as a tool, but Sam never thought it would actually *work.* She gave an experimental sniff and that was all it took to set Josh off again.

"You deserve that promotion. You're the best, Sam. You are. I'll tell Hennesey that. I'll tell him anything you want me to. I'll offer to give free seminars—well, no, sorry, can't do that, but I'll do something."

Sam rolled her eyes. Even in guilt, he was typical Josh.

"I know you hate me right now, but you've got to let me help you."

Listen to that. Incredible. "But...but what can you do?" Sam gave her voice the trademark Fiery Femmes quiver.

"I'll make you look good. I'll make Leonard Sheffield look like the wimp he is. I'll expose Wannerstein—somewhere, somebody has got something on that guy. I'll find it."

Shifting in the seat, Sam gave a tremulous sigh and looked over at him. "Thank you, Josh."

"Don't worry, Sam. I'll take care of you."

Big strong man and his little woman. Sam was surprised she didn't throw up all over Claire's sweater. Still, seeing this side of Josh would help the time pass until they got to New York. And after that, boy, would she let him have it. Talk about unzinging.

Sam readjusted the shoulder harness and drew her knees up. Propping her elbow against the headrest, she gave another small sniff. Mustn't overdo it. "Harvey is probably too much for me, but if I, say, wanted to make Leonard look like a wimp, what could I do?"

AT LEAST SHE WAS STILL talking to him. Josh surreptitiously held his damp palms over the air-conditioning vents. He didn't do well around crying females. His mother and sisters never cried, at least not in front of him, and due to the keep-it-light nature of his relationships, he had limited experience with women's waterworks.

Sam crying. What had they done to her? It must have been the stress. No telling what shape she would have been in if she'd stayed the whole two weeks. He was right to get her out of there.

Realization set in. *He'd virtually kidnapped her.* He'd broken—no smashed...cut, actually—rules here. Stupid, but serious rules.

There would be consequences, but he hadn't thought that far ahead yet.

What had he done? What had he been thinking? More important, what was *Sam* thinking?

He slid another look at her, one in a long line of many. He couldn't *stop* looking at her and he'd tried. If he wasn't with her, he was thinking about her. If he *was* with her, he couldn't stop looking at her. This was not good. Sam was an attractive woman and he'd always acknowledged that. But at some point tonight she'd started looking...looking...well, something. Something more than usual. Dangerously more.

Sam crossed her legs and that skirt of hers slid up her thighs even more. Even after her legs had stopped moving, that skirt kept slithering upward as though it was alive—

"Josh!"

He jerked the car back to the center of the lane. Yeah, she was dangerous all right. He was *not* going to look at her again. He was going to keep his eyes firmly, if reluctantly, on the road.

WHAT WAS WITH HIM? He'd nearly run them off the road. Sam recrossed her legs, liking the way the skirt caressed her skin.

Josh audibly swallowed and gripped the steering wheel.

Well, well, well. So he wasn't as immune to the skirt as he pretended. Good skirt. She patted it.

For the last couple of hours he'd been giving her all sorts of strategies for dealing with Leonard and Harvey and they'd been trading stories of their greatest sales triumphs.

She'd about used up hers and although she knew he could keep talking, he'd graciously refrained.

"So where are you from, Josh?" she asked out of the blue.

"Why?"

"Well, we're stuck in this car and I realize that I don't know anything about your background."

"It's a little late for that, isn't it?"

Sam was trying the men-love-to-talk-about-themselves tack. It figured that Josh would be the exception to the rule. "Forget it. I was just making conversation."

"Make some other conversation."

"Why?"

"I don't have conversations about that."

Sam eyed him. "Well, now I'm all curious. What are you hiding?"

"I'm not *hiding* anything. It's just not stuff that comes up when I talk to people."

In that case, there was no sense in gently leading up to the big question. "Have you ever been married?" She didn't have to ask if he was married now. Nothing about Josh said "married."

"No."

"Ever come close?"

"No."

"Ever wanted—"

"No."

"No wonder nobody asks about your background."

Several seconds went by before Josh spoke. "Have you?"

"Have I what?"

"You know, been married."

"Nope. I was close, but it didn't work out." And the only regret she felt was that Kevin had been hurt, but since she'd come to New York, she'd barely given him a thought. In fact, she'd thought about Josh a thousand times more often than she'd ever thought about Kevin. That wasn't to say she thought loving thoughts about Josh, either. No, they were mostly furious thoughts, thoughts of revenge...and, to her annoyance, the odd lustful thought or two. Or ten. "Still, I'd like to be married some day," she added.

She saw his gaze shift her way, then dart back to the road. "Good for you," he said.

"Just not anytime soon." Why was she telling him this? "With all the travel, it's hard to sustain a relationship." Except there wasn't *that* much travel and a relationship was always work. But the excuse sounded good.

Sam shifted so she could study him.

"You're staring at me."

"Just trying to figure you out. Who is Josh Crandall? Mild-mannered convention salesman..." she dropped her voice, "...or more?"

"Cut it out, Sam."

"But why? You've suddenly become intriguingly mysterious."

"There's nothing..." Exhaling, he muttered something she couldn't hear. "I'm from Kansas City.

Mother, father, two sisters. Here." He dug out his wallet. "There's a picture."

Sam found herself eager for this glimpse into Josh's personal life. The wallet he handed her was warm from his body and was slightly curved to the shape of his hip.

She held it a moment, feeling a strange intimacy with Josh. Then she turned on the dome light in the car, opened the wallet and quickly checked his driver's license. He was who he said he was, according to the document, and was three years older than she was.

Then she saw the picture. It had been taken one Christmas, since Josh and his family were posed in front of a decorated tree. There was Josh, smiling widely at the camera, his arms draped across the shoulders of two unsmiling young women. Next to them, was his mother, also unsmiling, and a man who could only be Josh's dad, still handsome, still with the megawatt smile.

Sam didn't have to be a body language expert to see the stiff way Josh's sisters held themselves, or how Josh was attempting to fake a closeness that wasn't there.

He was an incredibly good-looking man—clearly inheriting his father's smile and his mother's eyes and dark brows. But, so had his sisters. In fact, they looked exactly like Josh. But while the movie-star square jaw and strong masculine features made him look attractive, these same features didn't translate well to the female face. Josh's sisters were, in a word, plain. No, it was going to take two words: severely plain. They weren't trying, either. They wore no makeup and had pulled their hair back exactly like Josh's mother.

"Your sisters look just like you." Sam had to say something and was grateful to think of that.

"So people always say. They're lawyers," he added, pride evident in his voice.

"Are they married?" Sam asked faintly.

"No. They're too busy trying to make partner."

"Do you get to see your family much?"

"The usual holidays." His voice was flat.

Sam closed his wallet and handed it back to him. The picture had told her a lot about Josh, more than she'd expected to learn from casual chitchat. If he'd known how revealing the photo was, she suspected he'd never have shown her.

Josh's outgoing personality was evident, even in a photograph. His mother and sisters were clearly more subdued—bitter, even. It showed in their expressions and in the lines around their mouths. Josh probably didn't get along with them and couldn't figure out why. That was the reason he didn't like talking about his family.

Sam felt an unwilling sympathy. She didn't want to feel sympathy while she was still mad at him.

And she *was* angry. She'd wasted an entire week of her life because of him and he would pay. Soon.

He cleared his throat. "Your turn."

She grinned. "Why, Josh. Are you actually inquiring about my family?"

"I wouldn't want to be impolite."

"Oh." She stared at the stars outside the window. They were so much brighter away from the city lights.

"So?"

"I wouldn't want to bore you."

"I asked, didn't I?"

"No. You said something about turns and not wanting to be impolite."

She saw him grit his teeth before saying, "Tell me about your family."

"You're still not asking."

"Are you going to tell me about your family, or not?"

"Maybe not. You don't really seem interested."

"I'm interested. I'm panting for details. You must tell all."

Sam laughed at his deadpan voice. "I've got three sisters. I'm the youngest."

"Okay, that's enough details."

He made her laugh again. "I'm just getting started. My parents divorced when I was nine and my mom, who's one of the original bra burners, raised us to be independent. We were supposed to be the generation that achieved equality with men."

He nodded. "You know, there *is* something to this family background discussion. I've got you all figured out now. No wonder you're so aggressive."

"Please. If I were a man, you wouldn't say that."

"Well, you're not and I am. What do your sisters do?"

"Pat's a teacher. Mom didn't like that. Too traditionally female. Next is Jo. She dropped out of medical school and became a nurse who married a doctor. Mom went around screaming cliché about that one. Chris is nearest my age."

"Do you all have guy names?"

"Mom thought it would help in the business world.

Chris is or was a bank vice president. Mom liked that because she thought Chris was in a good position to break through the glass ceiling, but she's pregnant again and she really wants to quit and stay home with her kids."

"So why doesn't she?" He glanced at her, then away.

"Well, she is, but Mom..." How could Sam explain without making her mother sound worse than she was? "Mom just doesn't want us to end up trapped."

"Wow. Are you ever easy to figure out. You want that promotion for your mother."

"Hey, I want it for me, but there's nothing wrong with Mom enjoying it, too."

"Your mother needs to go out and break her own glass ceilings and stop living through you and your sisters," he pronounced.

"You know, I agree with you on one hand, but the climate was different when she started working."

"So what's stopping her now?"

Sam considered the question and not for the first time. "Well, it's a little late in life for her and besides, she baby-sits Jo and Chris's kids while they work."

"Okay." He nodded. "She's made a choice. Just be sure she's not making your choice for you."

Sam didn't like him analyzing her. "Thank you, Dr. Crandall."

"No charge."

Shortly after that, as the glow of the city lights on the horizon became brighter, Sam remembered that she couldn't go back to the apartment. A.J. had met a cute detective—unfortunately also named Sam—and wanted to keep her options open. Roommates showing up unexpectedly were very bad for options.

"Josh, you're going to have to take me to a hotel." She dug in her purse.

"The Carrington?"

"No." She needed to plan what she was going to say to Hennesey first. "Some other place. Where is my...great. I need to use your cell phone. Mine's a hostage back at Fiery Femmes."

"I'll get your phone back for you." He made it sound like a quest.

"You're right about that. But in the meanwhile, I can't go to the apartment. I'm not supposed to be there and one of my roommates is entertaining this weekend. Besides it's the middle of the night, and I wouldn't want to frighten anyone." She emphasized that last part.

"I'm not going to take you to a hotel. You can spend the rest of the night at my place."

Oh, really. The opportunity for revenge might come sooner than she thought. She made a mild protest. "I can't inconvenience you like that."

"Oh, no. You're the one who's been inconvenienced. It's just for a few hours."

"Well, if you're sure..."

Sam mentally patted herself on the back. This couldn't have worked out better if she'd set it up herself.

9

JOSH'S PLACE TURNED OUT to be a slightly shabby furnished one-bedroom apartment he was renting by the week. Except for the weekly rental, it was typical New York. Since Sam was currently living in untypical New York luxury, she appreciated the skirt's powers even more. Now, if it would only work on Josh. She gave it a little twitch.

But Josh proved resistant, probably because he wouldn't even look at her. He'd never avoided looking at her before, but that was okay. It was only a matter of time.

"Can I get you something to eat?" he asked after hauling both her suitcases up four flights of stairs.

"I'm fine." Sam arranged herself on the couch, tucking her legs beneath her.

"Drink?"

She really didn't want anything, but she nodded. "I don't suppose you have tea?"

"Nah. I'm not much of a tea drinker." He'd disappeared behind the counter and had opened the refrigerator. "Beer?"

Ick. Beer at midnight. "Sounds great."

Sam all but hummed to herself as Josh opened two bottles. Anytime now, he'd make his move, and when he did, she was going to reject him in such a way that he'd embrace celibacy for the rest of his natural born days.

SHE'D WANTED TO GO TO A hotel, but had he taken her to a hotel? Oh, no. He'd taken her *here*. Now she was here. And he was here. They were both here. In the same place. At the same time. He couldn't get away from her. She'd curled up on his sofa like a pink-and-black cat looking all soft and in need of petting—uh, comforting.

He pulled two beers out of the fridge and opened them. Should he pour them into glasses? No, that would be too much like this was a date.

This wasn't a date, this was...was...letting a friend crash on the sofa after being kidnapped, that's what it was.

Carrying the beers, he rounded the corner from the kitchen and the full force of Sam's presence hit him.

At that moment, Samantha Baldwin was everything he'd ever wanted or would ever want in a woman, want being the operative word.

She'd thrown her head back as she massaged her neck and his eyes traced the line of her neck down her throat and over the fuzzy curves revealed by a most excellent sweater. The sweater was made for touching. It invited stroking and nuzzling and hugging and all things soft and warm. It was the kind of sweater that would crackle with static electricity in the winter, especially as it was removed.

Sam's chest gently rose and fell and Josh realized that it had been doing so for some time. She was aware that he was watching her—or more specifically staring at her chest. There was only so much chest-staring a woman would allow—in Josh's experience not a whole lot—before she objected. He swallowed. Sam hadn't objected. Why hadn't she objected? She should object, dammit!

He met her eyes, which were regarding him above a mouth curved in a Mona Lisa smile. Her hands slowly smoothed their way down her thighs, drawing Josh's gaze. She had on a soft black skirt that outlined her legs as though they were immortalized in bronze.

She looked like a World War II pinup photo.

She looked good. Too good.

Josh broke out in a cold sweat, just like the beer bottles. Any second and his only thoughts would be those concerning the ancestral prime directive to continue the human race.

He gripped the beer bottles and concentrated on the wet cold. He could do this. He'd done it before and he'd do it again. Or not do it. Yeah. That was the plan. Too bad he couldn't write down the plan where he could frequently refer to it in the next few minutes.

Pasting on a casual, yeah-you're-spending-the-night-so-what? smile, he strode over to the sofa. "Here you go." He handed Sam the beer and a coaster, then sat at the far end of the sofa and stretched out his legs. "Long day." He tilted his beer in her direction, then drank.

"You can say that again." Sam stretched her legs, too, but somehow, it brought her closer to him, which hadn't been the plan at all.

If he moved away, he'd look nervous. He definitely wasn't nervous. He was concerned, that's all. Concerned that he'd be tempted to take advantage of the situation.

Sam apparently had no such concerns. In a maneuver he couldn't decipher, she oozed across the sofa until she was within touching distance.

"Is anything here yours?"

Josh shook his head.

"Where is your stuff?"

"I don't have a lot of stuff. I travel light."

"Where's your home?"

"Here."

She wrinkled her forehead. Wrinkles had never looked so cute. "All the time?"

"No."

"Well, where is your home when you aren't here?"

Why was she asking all these hard questions? He was finding it difficult to think. "I guess I consider home where my parents live."

Her lips curved. She had white teeth. Luscious lips. A living toothpaste commercial. "You live with your parents?"

"Not exactly."

Sam gave him an exasperated look. "Okay, where do you get your mail?"

Who cared? "I'm having it forwarded here. I had a P.O. box at the Meckler in Chicago. I stayed in a room there. I guess that was home base."

She was staring at him, slowly moving her thumb up and down on the beer bottle. His eyes followed the movement and he swallowed. Without breaking the rhythm, she tilted the bottle to her lips and sipped daintily, then touched her tongue to the mouth of the bottle to catch a wayward drop, all the time holding his fascinated gaze with hers.

Ancestral rumblings pounded through his head and elsewhere. Particularly elsewhere. Make that *especially* elsewhere, an elsewhere that didn't operate according to plans.

Josh wished he'd taken those notes because right now, Sam was looking really good and, frankly, his plan details were getting real fuzzy. Like that sweater.

She was doing the thumb thing again. Did she know what she was doing? Of course she knew what she was doing. This was Sam. He looked to the ceiling as he sipped his beer, then risked meeting her eyes, just to prove that he could.

"You have no permanent home," she said.

They were still talking about that? With a herculean effort, Josh managed a casual "What's the point? I'm always moving around. Or I was. I guess I'll headquarter Perfect Pitch here in New York." He grinned. "I've invested too much in letterhead and brochures with the New York P.O. box."

Sam pointed to the boxes stacked in the dining area. "Are those your brochures?"

He nodded. Yeah, it didn't look too great, but he was the only one who was going to see the mess. "And the manuals and proposal packets. I have class materials printed up as needed. There's no sense in paying for storage and this way I can update as I learn what's effective and what isn't."

Sam looked interested and her hands were still as she listened, so Josh kept talking, letting down his guard since the conversation was on the presumably safe topics of course materials and brochures.

Mistake.

Sam scooted closer and looked up at him through lowered lashes. "That was sweet of you to rescue me, Josh."

Whoa. How did they get from brochures to gratitude? He straightened, coincidentally moving a few inches toward the arm of the sofa.

Sam only gave him that soft, sweet smile that made him want to fill his arms with her. And...and did she know that the top button of her sweater had come undone? When had that happened? How had that happened?

Josh drained his beer. Was it beer? For all the effect it had, he might as well have been drinking water. He needed some numbing effect against Sam.

She'd set her almost full beer on the coffee table. Was she going to drink it? Could he?

"And look. You ripped your shirt." She touched his sleeve. "You probably caught it on the fence."

No. There would be no touching. He pulled his arm away. "It's no big deal."

She moved right next to him and took his arm. "Let me see that. You might have scratched the skin." She set his arm down and gently probed at the place just below his elbow.

A roaring filled Josh's ears. His hand was on her silk-clad thigh. Her warm, silk-clad thigh. Her hair was just under his nose and her pink sweater with the unbuttoned button dipped ever so slightly outward. Slightly, because the thing was like a furry pink skin. But slightly was more than enough.

Josh felt like he was coming down with the flu.

"Have you had a tetanus shot recently?" she asked through moist, pink lips. Lips that were kissing distance away.

"I have no idea," he said. "But I should probably find out. That's a good idea. Thanks for saying something because it sure wouldn't have occurred to me. You know, I'm probably due for one, because I don't think I've had one since scout camp and that had to be, what fifteen, twenty years ago? My, God, it's twenty years! I can't believe it." Babbling, babbling. But babbling lips weren't kissing lips.

Sam raised an eyebrow. "Neither can I. But don't get in a panic. I didn't see any blood. Yet."

"Well, that's a relief." Josh stood, knowing that he had to get away from her and her fuzzy pinkness.

He could barely stand. Everything in him screamed to grab her and never let go. But that was totally absurd. What would he do with her? Short-term, no problem. But he had to think long-term with Sam, since they'd already established that she wasn't a short-term person. As she so recently pointed out, he didn't even have a real home.

What was going on here? They'd been talking tetanus shots, not marriage.

Marriage. He had a dizzy moment. The beer was stronger than he thought. Josh plucked both bottles off the coffee table and set them on the kitchen bar, then headed for the bedroom closet.

"It's getting late. I'll make up the sofa if you want to use the bathroom," he called and grabbed some sheets.

She was still sitting on the sofa when he dumped the sheets on a chair. The green-and-white Meckler logo marched across the edge.

Sam glanced at them. "Only the very best, I see."

"Wait until you see the towels."

She wasn't moving. Well, neither would he.

They stared at each other.

This wasn't working. Josh could feel himself being drawn to her. Just because he had to have something in his hands and it had better not be Sam, Josh pulled the side pillow off the sofa.

Sam stretched, arms flung over her head.

Josh gripped the pillow—an ugly brown, tan, and yellow plaid—and drew an unsteady breath.

"I *am* getting sleepy," she announced and mercifully uncurled herself from the sofa.

Josh studiously avoided looking at her while she unzipped her suitcase behind him. Concentrating fiercely, he tucked the sheets around the sofa as she padded across the room.

"I'll just be a minute." She closed the bathroom door.

Josh sagged. He was exhausted from the effort of maintaining a purely platonic state between them when everything in him raged for a Sam orgy.

He needed to stick to the plan. He had to keep telling himself that this was all one sided. His side. He'd broken into her room and dragged her back to New York and insisted that she stay in his apartment. She was under his protection. There was a code about this sort of thing.

The bathroom door opened and Josh forgot all about codes and plans.

Sam stood there with nothing between them except a very thin cotton T-shirt.

Very thin. He'd just guessed about the cotton.

The light behind her outlined her body. His mouth went dry. He just stared at her, unable to look away. He concentrated on dragging air into his lungs and could see his chest rise and fall.

He could see her chest rise and...and there wasn't much falling.

"Um, here. Good night." Josh made it to his bedroom and closed the door, leaning against it, his heart pounding.

What he needed, what he really needed was a cold shower. Using the bathroom entrance from his bedroom, he locked the other door and stripped off his clothes.

He turned the shower on and stepped inside, and just as quickly stepped back out. Cold showers weren't for him. As the water warmed, he smelled a floral fragrance and saw that Sam had left a bottle of creamy stuff on the sink.

Great. He couldn't even get away from her in here.

Moaning, he rested his head against the shower wall and let the water beat against his shoulders. What was the plan again? Oh, yeah. Avoid Sam because she'd hate him if he didn't and then he'd never see her again. This way, they could be...what? Friends?

Stupid plan.

After quickly showering, he pulled on a pair of boxers and climbed into bed. Like he was going to sleep anytime soon.

Two seconds later, Sam knocked on his door. "Josh?"

He bolted out of bed, glad that he'd skipped the cold shower because the effects sure wouldn't have lasted long.

Josh pulled the door open about two inches. "What?"

"Do you have an extra pillow?"

"Just a minute." He took one of the two off his bed and pushed it through the doorway.

Sam gasped. "Your arm! You did scratch it!"

From her reaction, it sounded as though he'd nearly amputated it.

She pulled him through the door and switched on the lamp by the sofa. "Look at that."

The scratch was nothing more than a short thin red line, but that wasn't the point. The point was that Sam and her very flimsy see-through T-shirt was standing inches away from Josh and his very bare chest.

She looked up at him.

He looked down at her.

She moved her hand up his arm toward his shoulder.

He squeezed his eyes shut, the feel of her fingers against his skin nearly doing him in. With a superhuman strength he didn't know he possessed, Josh took hold of her wrist before her hand could slide around the back of his neck and pulled her arm down.

He opened his mouth to say something, anything, when she captured his hand and drew it to her breast.

He went nearly incoherent as he was flooded with a long-suppressed desire.

The weight of her breast was heavy in his palm and for many moments he savored the feel of her, his eyes locked on hers.

His thumb was an inch from the T-shirt's neckline. Drawing his thumb back and forth across the soft skin of her throat, he watched as Sam caught her bottom lip in her teeth. Standing on tiptoe, she encircled her arms around his neck and this time he didn't stop her. Couldn't stop her.

She leaned into the kiss and he kissed her back. He knew better but was counting on his strong sense of self-preservation to save him before he was lost. Her mouth opened wide beneath his and he wondered if he might already be lost.

But when she dipped her fingers beneath the waistband of his boxers, his self-preservation finally kicked in.

"Sam, no." He placed his hands on hers. "I can't."

"And I have evidence that you can."

Josh took a step backward, then forced himself to take another until her hands fell away. "Sam, we've been through a stressful experience together and I know you're grateful to me, but I think you'd have some regrets tomorrow morning."

She drew her eyebrows together. "Josh..."

He backed toward the bedroom. "What you're feeling is very common among women who've been rescued. Emotions are heightened because of all the leftover adrenaline, but acting on those emotions isn't the best idea."

Sam stood—and it would be in front of the light—looking at him with an unreadable expression.

It was best that he not try to analyze it. "Good night." He'd slipped through the door between "good" and "night" and now he shut it.

Josh climbed into bed and tried not to think of Sam out there.

Out there. Sam shouldn't be out there. She should be in here and he should be out there.

He grabbed his pillow and went out into the living room. "Sam?"

"Josh?" She hadn't moved.

"Sam, you take the bed. I'll sleep out here."

"But I'm fine—"

"Please go into the bedroom."

"Okay, okay." She took the pillow and stomped past him, slamming the door.

"Lock it," he called. It was very important that she lock it.

Josh heard the bolt snap, then lay on the couch and groaned. It was still warm from Sam's body. He could smell that lotion she'd used.

And, of course, now he had to grapple with thoughts of Sam in his bed while he wasn't.

It was going to be a long night.

OF ALL THE NERVE. Sam couldn't believe that sanctimonious little speech Josh had given her last night. Telling her it was normal for women to have the hots for their rescuers. Rescuer—ha! Hots—double ha! As though she'd flung herself at him when *he* was the one panting after *her*. She knew panting when she heard it. She'd almost reduced him to a mental amoeba when he'd rejected her before she could reject him.

So now she needed revenge for the failed revenge.

Sam flung on her clothes and scribbled a quick "Thanks" on a Perfect Pitch brochure—the only paper she could find. Avoiding looking at the lump on the sofa—make that snoring lump on the sofa—she crept out of Josh's apartment.

Back in her very own temporary apartment, she planned her revenge. She also had to figure out what she was going to tell Mr. Hennesey. And she'd better call Fiery Femmes before *they* called Hennesey. Thank you so much, Josh.

The call to Fiery Femmes was easy. Sam faked an "urgent personal matter" and they accepted it. Apparently their clients had a lot of "urgent personal matters." They agreed to mail back her cell phone.

She started to call Hennesey, then stopped. She wasn't expected back until later in the week. Maybe she didn't want to go back right away.

Maybe she wanted to give the Family Values folks another try—complete with quivery voice and tearful apology. What could it hurt?

JOSH WOKE UP, REALIZED HE had a serious Sam hangover, called in sick, and went back to sleep.

HALF AN HOUR AND ONE call to the Family Values Assembly later, Sam was doing a victory dance around the apartment when A.J. emerged from the bedroom and stopped cold. "I thought you were Claire. What are you doing back?"

Sam told her about Josh and was gratified by the look on A.J.'s face.

"That guy has it bad for you." A.J. poured a mug of coffee and put an ice cube in it.

Sam shook her head. "Trust me, he doesn't. But listen to this. I used some Fiery Femmes stuff, the quivery voice and a little crying—"

"You didn't!"

"Hey, it works. You ought to try it."

"I'll pass." A.J. gulped the rest of her coffee, rinsed her mug and collected her portfolio.

"Anyway, I called Family Values and guess what? They're having a regional meeting right here in New York and said I could meet with them."

"Congratulations. Hey, listen, as long as you're back, could I borrow the skirt?"

Sam was feeling magnanimous. "Sure."

"Thanks!"

A yawning Claire emerged from the study right after A.J. left. "Hey, you're back."

Sam went through her story again.

Claire's reaction was more subdued probably because she was all but sleepwalking. "That's great, Sam." She yawned. "Sorry. I was out until two a.m."

"Go back to bed and I'll walk Cleo." Sam hoped Claire would argue with her, but she didn't.

"Thanks." Claire shuffled back to the study. "Oh— can I borrow the skirt?"

"Yeah, I just want it for my Family Values meeting."

"'Kay." Claire shut the door.

Sam got her keys and quietly slipped out the door.

She was in such a good mood that even walking Cleo wouldn't spoil it.

CONCERNING MR. HENNESEY, Sam decided to go with the old a-best-defense-is-a-good-offense route.

"Hi, Mr. Hennesey!" Sam pasted on a perky Fiery Femmes smile as she knocked on his door later that morning. "I'm back early."

"Sam! Come in."

Sam walked in talking. "Josh came up to Fiery Femmes for a midcourse assessment and we realized that I'd already learned all the new material during the first week and that second week was just reinforcement. Josh felt that was excessive and I concurred, so he gave me a ride back."

"Good." Hennesey accepted her carefully scripted explanation. "I understand he's not feeling well today."

"We got back really late last night and he wasn't looking all that great." Sam enjoyed saying that. She figured Josh had slept as little as she had. The difference was that she was jazzed from the Family Values call. Time to drop that on Mr. Hennesey. "By the way, I gave Family Values a call and have a meeting with them Friday."

"Excellent. I hope you can mend some fences there."

Interesting choice of words. "I'll do my best." And if all went according to plan, her best would be better than Josh's best.

THERE WAS JUST ONE SMALL blip in Sam's plan. Both A.J. and Claire wanted to borrow the skirt the day Sam had planned to wear it for her Family Values meeting.

"But you wore it last night!" Claire said to A.J. on Friday morning.

"And I need it again tonight," A.J. insisted. They were all in her room.

Sam had retrieved the skirt from A.J.'s closet and was zipping it up. "What time do you need it?" She really only needed to wear the skirt during her presentation to the FVA board.

"Detective Romano is picking me up at five."

Sam nodded. "I can meet you here by five and we'll exchange skirts. You've got that black knockoff I can wear."

She and A.J. looked at Claire who was rubbing her temple. "If I could have the skirt some time during Petra's gallery showing tonight, that would work for me."

"Okay," A.J. told her and Claire smiled in relief.

"So we're all set?" Sam asked.

"Except for the pink blouse you're wearing," A.J. said.

Sam glanced down at herself. "I have to look soft and feminine."

"Yeah, but you're going to have to sneak past Franco," Claire said.

"Believe me, sneaking past Franco is the *least* of my challenges today."

But Sam should have known that she couldn't sneak anything past Franco.

"*What* are you wearing?" He shaded his eyes the instant she got off the elevator.

"I know it's horrible, but I've got to wear pink today. I thought with the black jacket and skirt it wouldn't be so bad." She hoped he'd tell her it didn't look too bad.

"You look very retro. A suggestion—pin a deep pink flower to your lapel. That way you'll have the right color next to your face."

The man was brilliant. "Good idea. Thanks, Franco!"

Flowers were feminine, too. And today was all about being feminine.

"And Sam," he pleaded, "I'm desperate for gossip. Everyone else here is going through a dull spell."

"I'll do my best."

Sam practiced quivering and stammering and lowering her lashes all the way to the hotel where the Family Values regional meeting was being held.

She had a few rough moments when she first walked into the room, but she gave the men a tremulous smile. "Thank you so much for seeing me. I—I was afraid you wouldn't and then...well, I almost l-lost my job..."

Oops. One of those quivers wasn't fake. But anyway, it didn't matter. As soon as Sam finished telling them how scared she was about losing her job, she knew she had them.

HOWEVER, GETTING THEM TO make a decision took forever and when Sam raced through the lobby, A.J.'s date was right behind her. Fortunately, Franco sized up the situation and distracted him.

"I can't believe you're late!" A.J. stood by the apartment door in her slip and practically ripped the skirt off Sam.

"Sorry. They kept asking questions." Sam pulled on

A.J.'s skirt. "I've got to run back there. The Family Values folks think I'm checking in with the office. Oh, and by the way, the cute detective with my favorite name arrived at the same time I did. He's pacing back and forth with Franco in the lobby."

A.J. zipped the skirt and turned in a full circle. "What do you think?"

Boy, she must really like the guy. "I think that the cute detective is in deep trouble."

"I hope so." A.J. took a couple of steps toward the door, then turned back. "I really hope so."

Sam grinned at her.

"I...you're sure you don't need the skirt?"

Taking her hands, Sam said, "I'm positive. Go for it."

Nodding, A.J. inhaled, then glanced at her watch. "At seven I'm handing the skirt off to Claire. I feel like I'm in a relay."

So did Sam. "I'm just happy that my lap is over."

"Wish me luck." A.J. literally ran out the door.

Sam fastened the skirt, checked her makeup and was right behind her.

"WE'RE IMPRESSED WITH THE proposal, Ms. Baldwin. We very much like the idea of Washington, D.C." Mr. Carelle nodded to his colleagues. "So much so, that we will consider invoking our cancellation clause in order to hold our next convention at the Carrington there. We will have to vote on this after the dinner break. Several of our regional colleagues are arriving for tonight's reception. Could you be there in case they have further questions?"

What else could anyone possibly ask? They'd grilled her all afternoon. "Of course," Sam assured them.

It figured that the FVA board would throw a kink into her plans. Claire was scheduled to wear the skirt tonight, but Sam didn't know for how long. If she were lucky, it wouldn't be for all night.

SAM RACED BACK TO THE apartment. She absolutely had to get out of her shoes. They were killing her feet.

No one was home when she hobbled into the apartment. Great. Claire was probably still at Petra's gallery showing. Sam kicked off her shoes and contemplated calling A.J.'s cell phone to find out just exactly where the gallery was, but when she walked into her room, she saw a skirt on her bed.

Sam exhaled in relief. Thank goodness. That *was* the skirt, wasn't it? She held it up to the light. It sure looked like it. Sam took off A.J.'s skirt and changed into this one, found some black pumps with lower heels and prepared to face the Family Values board one more time.

10

JOSH HADN'T SEEN Sam all week. That didn't mean he didn't constantly watch for her. Or think about her.

Or do things for her. Leonard Sheffield had come up with some grandiose plan to impress Hennesey that Josh casually blasted out of the water. It was almost too easy. He should have used more finesse but he'd wanted to squash Sheffield for Sam. Now he'd made an enemy.

So if he counted Sam, that meant he now had two enemies. But, was that enough? Oh, no. He repeated a few rumors about Wannerstein that had the Carrington brass looking into some of his past dealings. Wannerstein wasn't stupid. He'd figure out what had happened and so now Josh guessed he had three enemies.

And was Sam around to appreciate what he'd done for her? No. She was obviously avoiding him.

They were going to have to talk, and soon, because Josh didn't want her for an enemy. He just wanted her.

SHE'D DONE IT. Family Values was canceling with Meckler and going with Carrington.

It was after eight when Sam practically skipped back to the office. Although nothing was "signed, sealed and delivered" as Mr. Hennesey liked to say, she had a verbal agreement. And if you couldn't trust the word of the Family Values Assembly, who could you trust?

Sam was running on pure elation and wanted to write a memo reporting on her meeting to Mr. Hennesey before she crashed for the evening. Maybe she'd visit the pastry chef and see if he had any leftover goodies. Something rich and sweet would be just the thing for bribing her roommates into telling about their skirt experiences. Sam smoothed down the fabric. The skirt was her lucky charm, It was going to be hard to give it up, but she couldn't be selfish about it, especially since if she got this promotion, and her chances were looking pretty good right now, she wouldn't have time to deal with any men the skirt attracted.

Tiffany had left for the day, which was too bad since Sam wanted her to know that she was out of the doghouse. Sam checked for messages at the reception desk in case Family Values had called. Nothing there, so she headed toward her cubicle. Just as she reached for the light switch, a voice came out of the darkness.

"Hey, Sam."

The adrenaline burst wasn't so bad this time. She flipped on the light. Josh sat in her chair, feet propped on her desk, fingers laced behind his head.

She ignored the feet on the desk bit since he was only doing that to annoy her. "Josh? Now what are you doing?"

"Waiting for you." There was no Josh smile.

He knew. Incredibly, he knew. One of the FVA board members must have called him already.

Sam felt deflated. Half—more than half—the fun of stealing Family Values was getting to tell Josh. But she'd wanted revenge, now she had revenge. At least for this. "So here I am."

"Yeah." He unlaced his fingers and lowered his feet. "I had some news for you and since I couldn't reach you on your cell phone—"

"They're mailing it back." She didn't like the tone in his voice. It was larger and deeper than just plain anger.

"Good." He continued to look at her. It was a weird expression, as though he hated her and yet was having trouble keeping his hands off her.

Conflict. Good. "What did you want to tell me?"

"Just that I took out Sheffield for you. Wannerstein is still standing, but might be mortally wounded."

That was a surprise. "Thanks." She wasn't going to ask what he'd done. Or why.

He nodded, that strange look still in his eyes. "So while I'm risking my career for you, I find you're doing something for me as well."

Okay. He was angry, that's what it was. Blazingly angry. And...hurt? Couldn't be. This was Josh and this was the revenge she'd wanted. Time to finish it so he'd think twice about treating her as a powerless neophyte. "I felt I should apologize for offending the Family Values board. You would have been proud. I used all the Fiery Femmes techniques I learned."

She watched as the point struck home. Except for the barest flicker of his eyelids, his expression didn't change. "They fell all over themselves trying to make poor little me feel better. They even let me give my presentation again. I think they liked it."

"You know they did."

She let a beat go by. "Yeah, I do."

They stared at each other with Sam trying to savor her revenge and resenting Josh because she didn't. She should not feel guilty. He deserved every bit of this and more.

But Josh just kept looking at her with that strange glitter in his eyes. It unsettled her.

"Come on, Josh. You would have done the same thing."

He continued to stare at her and then a smile of acknowledgement slowly spread across his face. "You're right. I would have done exactly the same thing. Good job, kid."

She'd let the "kid" pass. She could be gracious in victory. "Let me buy you dinner." Though it was on the late side, she was suddenly hungry.

"Sounds good."

They tried to make reservations, but after calling four restaurants—even the Carrington was full—Josh suggested that they have dinner at his place. "You can cook."

"What makes you think I can cook?" she asked.

"Didn't they teach you at Fiery Femmes? Isn't that a womanly talent?"

Sam ignored the jab. "As a matter of fact, I spent some time in the kitchen with a chef. I don't think you want me cooking for twenty, though."

"Then I guess that leaves takeout."

Something, perhaps a long-dormant, long-suppressed, underdeveloped feminine nesting gene flickered to life within Sam. When was the last time Josh had eaten a home-cooked meal? Claire had been cooking when it was her turn and Sam had enjoyed the freshly prepared food. Besides, how hard could it be to grill a couple of chicken breasts? "No, I'll cook. What have you got in the fridge?"

"Beer and bagels. Maybe some orange juice."

The orange juice was more than she'd expected. "Looks like we're going shopping."

Outwardly, he appeared to be the old Josh, but he was in a strange mood. There was no sign of her guilty rescuer. Josh was friendly, but distant. Ever the professional. There might have been no history between them.

Except there was history between them and she could see the awareness of it in his eyes when he looked at her.

She considered them professionally even. Maybe they were and maybe they weren't, but she'd had enough revenge to soothe her ego. And by luring away Family Values, she'd demonstrated that she was his equal. That must be it. Josh was having a hard time accepting her as a peer. His pride was still bruised.

He needed to get over it.

When they got to the grocery near his apartment, Josh grabbed a plastic-handled shopping basket. "So what's for dinner?"

Sam had been thinking about this. There was a certain Jamaican seasoning the Fiery Femmes chef had used and she wanted to try that. "I was thinking grilled chicken breasts, wild rice, salad and strawberries. White wine, of course." Maybe a little pâté and crackers to nibble on while she cooked. Simple and elegant.

Josh made a disgusted sound as he prowled the aisles. "I wasn't thinking anything like that."

No, he was probably thinking pizza to go with his beer. All right. She could be flexible. He just needed to win a point against her. She should have anticipated that and suggested pizza and beer first so he could reject that. "Okay, how about some pasta with bread and salad?"

Josh gave her a look. "How about some meat, woman? I'm talking thick, bloody steaks and baked potatoes with the works. We do it right and there's no room on the plate for rabbit food. And for dessert one of those New York cheesecakes. Or apple pie. Yeah, apple pie with ice cream."

Pie from scratch was currently beyond Sam's culinary abilities. But, that's what bakeries were for.

Josh continued. "A meal like that deserves a wine you can taste. A red wine."

"A meal like that deserves a coronary-care unit on standby."

"Not if you don't make a habit of it." Josh had led her to the meat case and was pointing out two large slabs of meat. Two large slabs of meat at twelve ninety-eight a pound. "Isn't that the prettiest sight you've ever seen?"

Well, not exactly. But Sam understood. He wasn't letting her off cheap. Fine. She hadn't intended to skimp. This was her victory dinner. She nodded to the butcher. "Steak and baked potatoes isn't exactly cooking."

"That way you can concentrate on the mushroom sauce."

"What mushroom sauce?"

Josh accepted the white paper-wrapped package from the butcher. "You can't have steaks like these without mushrooms on the side. Don't you cook mushrooms?"

"Uh, no."

"I'll cook those, then."

Josh steered her toward the produce section, first selecting two monster potatoes, then heading for the mushrooms.

"But I'm supposed to be cooking for you." It was a mild protest. Sam wasn't into cooking.

"Don't worry about it. Go pick some sour cream, chives and bacon bits. Maybe some cheddar cheese while you're at it. And eggs for the mushroom batter."

Whatever, Sam thought.

JOSH WANTED TO HATE HER. He wanted to be angry. He wanted to pick a fight. He wanted her to go away and leave him alone. But if she did go away and leave him alone, he'd spend all his time thinking about her. So here he was, picking mushrooms instead.

Nothing good was going to come out of this evening.

Josh had broken all kinds of rules where Sam was concerned. Professional rules, personal rules—and there were always the legal rules.

And she...she hadn't been grateful. No, she'd acted exactly the way he would have—and had in the past. So why did it bother him so much? Why did she bother him so much? Why couldn't he stay away from her? She was everything he didn't want. Except he did.

Josh finished with the mushrooms and went over to

the wine section. They were headed for a showdown, he and Sam, and he had no idea what the outcome would be. He didn't even know what he *wanted* the outcome to be, just that there would inevitably be one.

Josh found one of his favorite merlots, a little on the pricey side, but Sam was paying.

Then again, he had a feeling he would be as well.

THE TENSION BETWEEN THEM was both strong and inexplicable. Sam struggled not to feel guilty over what she'd done and was irritated with Josh for his attitude. She accepted that he wasn't used to losing, but really.

When *she* was the one who'd been bested, he expected her to take it and move on. No hard feelings. But when someone got the better of him, watch out.

Oh, sure, he was trying to hide his resentment, but he wasn't trying very hard. And every once in a while, she caught him looking at her in a way that was neither detached, nor professional. Emotions swirled beneath the surface.

She'd forgotten that she was wearing the skirt, but quite honestly, there were stronger emotions at work here than those caused by the skirt.

And some of them were hers. Yeah, she had a little emotion swirling going on herself. What had Claire said? *Sam has to get him the same way he got her, then things will be equal between them again. What they do after that is up to them.* That wasn't quite what had happened, but things were definitely equal, as far as she was concerned. So it was time for the "what they do after" part.

So what were they going to do?

If possible, Josh's apartment looked even more impersonal in the waning evening light. The sofa was back to normal—even though its normal would send Franco screaming into the night—with no sign that Sam had ever been there.

There was no sign *Josh* had ever been there.

Sam shed her jacket and joined Josh in the cramped kitchen. He'd just opened the wine and had poured her a glass. When he handed it to her, she took a sip and asked, "Josh, are you still mad at me?" She'd just spent far too much money on good food for him to brood all evening.

Slowly, he raised his own glass and held it to the light, making the liquid glow a rich ruby. He swirled the wine, then brought the glass to his lips. "No." He drank, then lowered the glass.

And then he looked at her. Just looked.

But it was such a look. Revealing. Intense. Smoldering.

He almost didn't look like Josh anymore. It was as though he'd removed one of those translucent Halloween masks and she could see him more clearly. See the Josh behind the smile.

His eyes appeared bigger and Sam realized it was because they were usually narrowed in a smile. He looked not tired, but subdued and wary. And hungry. Hungry for her, she was gratified to see, but there was more. What did he want in return? Acceptance?

Affection.

Sam caught her breath. That was it. In her mind she saw the picture with his sour-faced mother and sisters and a father who stood off to the side. She saw Josh trying to gather them close to him as he smiled his big, all-encompassing smile.

But just when she started feeling sorry for him, the mask slipped back into place and all that was left was a frankly carnal look. No teasing. No smile.

Sam's mouth went dry, in spite of the excellent wine. Even if she hadn't seen the deeper expression, a look such as the one he was giving her now demanded acknowledgment.

One way or the other.

She took another sip of wine as she decided what she wanted to do.

The corners of his mouth turned up changing his smoldering look into a teasing one.

Sam couldn't believe it. She'd nearly fallen for Josh's act again. Okay, fine. He wanted to tease, let's see if he could take it.

Sam took another sip of wine and set the glass on the counter. "Want some pâté?" She was already opening the slab she'd bought at the deli.

"I don't know. I'm not much of a pâté person." He turned back to his precious mushrooms, stirring up some noxious batter for them.

"You'll like this." Sam arranged some crackers, then smeared one of them with the rich spread. She approached Josh, making sure to get into his space—that would teach him to call *her* bluff—and held the cracker to his lips until he opened his mouth.

She popped it in. "Oops. There's just a little bit here." There wasn't, but she used the opportunity to brush her fingers against his lower lip. "There." She smiled up at him, noting with satisfaction that he'd gone very still.

If she were being very truthful, she'd admit to feeling a little zing, herself. "Isn't that good?"

He nodded, zombielike, and turned back to the mushroom batter. "You can put the steaks under the broiler. Better turn it on first. I've never used it."

"What if it doesn't work?"

"Then we'll eat mushrooms, potatoes and—" he gestured with his shoulder "—that junk."

Sam started pulling open drawers. "I thought you liked that junk."

"It's okay."

"Want me to make you another cracker?"

"No! I mean, I'm saving myself for steak."

Sam smiled to herself. She found a tea towel and tied it around her waist to avoid getting anything on the skirt. She didn't know the rules for cleaning the thing or what would happen if it got grease spatters on it. The skirt did seem awfully subdued tonight, probably because it had already attracted Josh. Like that was a big challenge. Josh flirted with all females.

No, the poor thing was probably resting after the rigors of whatever A.J. and Claire had put it through, not to mention the stuffy Family Values men. Now *that* had been a challenge.

"Hey! Look what I found." Sam pulled out an apron with Kiss the Cook emblazoned across the bib. Giving Josh an impish look, she draped it over his head then tied it behind his back, ignoring the memory of a bare-chested Josh delivering his stupid I'm-going-to-be-strong-for-both-of-us speech.

Well, the bare-chested part was okay to remember, she decided.

"Don't get any ideas," he said.

"You wish."

"Kinda." He glanced at her. "But we both know it wouldn't be a good thing."

At least he admitted he was attracted to her. She could work with that. "Hey. Don't sell yourself short."

He gave her another look. "I never do."

Well. Teasing was all very fine and good, but she kept having to remind herself that it *was* only teasing and the purpose was to reject *him*.

Sam put the steaks under the broiler. "Is there something else I could be doing?"

"No. You just watch those."

"Okay." Some cook she was. Grabbing her wine, she hopped onto the bar where she had a good view of both Josh and the steaks.

He methodically cleaned and sliced the mushrooms, virtually ignoring her.

She couldn't have that, could she? Sam slid all the way onto the bar, turned and drew up one leg. The skirt slithered down her thigh. Draining her glass, she held it out. "Could I have some more wine, please?"

"Sure." Wiping his hands on a towel, Josh picked up the wine bottle, turned around and froze.

SAM SAT ON THE COUNTER and looked like sin personified. She knew it, too.

What she didn't know was how close to the edge Josh was. She'd haunted his dreams, both sleeping and waking. Over and over, he relived the feel of her, the moment when she'd put his hand on her breast and her lips on his mouth. And he'd thought it was bad the past two years when all he'd had was his imagination.

He knew Sam, knew the type of woman she was and knew she wanted something he couldn't give her. He needed to back away. Instead, he approached her and refilled her wineglass. The steaks sizzled and popped in the silence.

He wanted to touch her again. Would that be so horrible? Yes. It would also be really great.

He could smell the lotion or shampoo or whatever it was she used. It was an alien smell that had pervaded his space, a constant reminder that she'd been here before.

This was the worst kind of torture. He should never have suggested that they come here, but it had seemed inevitable. He finished pouring the wine and gave her a resigned look.

Before the night was through, they were either going to be lovers, or mortal enemies.

His money was on enemies.

Sam slid off the counter. "I'll check the steaks."

There wasn't a lot of room in the kitchen. Josh concentrated on slicing the mushrooms into perfect slices.

Sam pulled out the broiler and flipped the steaks, then stood and watched him. "Hennesey didn't mind that I was back early."

"So I heard."

"Thanks for coming to get me out of that place, Josh."

Her voice was all soft. "My pleasure." *My idiocy.*

"Seriously, I was impressed." She leaned over and

took a cracker, spread it with pâté and took a bite. She made another one and brought it to him.

He opened his mouth—the stuff was growing on him—and bit into the cracker. Her fingers lingered on his lips again before falling away.

"Shall I?"

Josh stared at the melting butter in the frying pan. "Shall you what?"

"Kiss the cook."

Desire hummed through his veins. "Sam," he said in halfhearted warning.

She swayed toward him and he thought his heart would burst through his chest. His only hope would be if he didn't touch her because once he did, there would be no stopping.

"You know, I'm not the same person I was two years ago," she said.

"Yes, you are." She always would be.

"We don't even work together anymore."

"We work together more than we did before."

"But it's only temporary."

Josh's breath was coming quickly and he felt light-headed. He handed her the potatoes. "Stick those in the microwave."

Mistake. Moving to the sink to scrub them brought her closer to him. He could feel the warmth of her body. The hair on his arms prickled.

Josh concentrated on slicing the last of the mushrooms.

Sam stabbed the potatoes with a fork and put them in the microwave. "You know, the rescue is over.

You've changed careers and I feel we're on an even footing. A level playing field, if you will."

"I won't." He ladled the mushrooms into the pan of melted butter. There was way too much batter.

"Why not?"

She was playing a game with him, but for him, it wasn't a game anymore. She'd seriously messed with his life. And he'd liked his life. It was exactly the way he wanted it: fast-paced, unencumbered and uninvolved. But for some reason, Sam kept *involving* him. He couldn't keep it simple or light with her. He did his job well because he kept his emotions out of it. Once emotions got into the negotiations, there went the edge.

Josh kept his edge finely honed.

Sam blunted it.

And now she was holding out hope when Josh knew that there was no hope. But as long as Sam acted as though there could be something between them, Josh couldn't stay away from her.

So, he'd have to see that she stayed away from him.

But of course, she didn't. "I asked why not?" She traced a finger around the *K* in Kiss the Cook.

Josh deliberately stepped around her and checked on the steaks. "You know, right now you're feeling really on top of the world because of the Family Values conference, but that was just luck." Nothing could get Sam madder quicker than criticizing her work.

She blinked and the steam started to rise. "I'd prepared a damned good presentation."

"Yeah, and then you went in there and wiggled your cute little butt at them while you gave them a sob story about losing your job. You found a new angle. Good for you. But it won't always work."

"Any butt wiggling I did, I learned at Fiery Femmes, which *you* sent me to."

"And that was the best thing that ever happened to you."

"Says you."

"Yeah, says me." The microwave dinged and Josh turned over the potatoes, then punched in a couple more minutes. "You needed some serious help." He was lying. Would she buy it?

Sam opened the cabinet, barely missing his head, and took out the plates. "I was doing just fine without your interference!"

"Only on the small-change conferences. You never landed a big one until you went after Family Values."

"The smaller ones can be even more profitable." After a glance at the dinette which was covered by his computer, she slammed the plates on the counter and went back for the silverware.

"You're only talking percentages, babe. Not the real bucks. If I hadn't smoothed the way for you, you wouldn't have a chance at your promotion."

"Smooth—!" Outrage made her cheeks flush. "I got here in *spite* of you! In spite of all your little tricks in getting conventions that should have gone to me."

"I made you work harder. You got better. But you've still got a long way to go until you're anywhere near my league." And that ought to do it.

But incredibly, it didn't.

Sam stared at him with her mouth open, then a thoughtful look crossed her face.

That couldn't be good. Josh dished out the food and set the plates on the counter.

Sam sat down and after a moment, she picked up a knife and sawed at the meat. "You're picking a fight with me."

Was he that transparent? "Just stating the facts, ma'am."

"The question is, why are you picking a fight? The steak is very good, by the way."

She was supposed to be furious at him, not enjoying her steak. It would have been a shame to waste the steak, though. Josh tried a piece. It *was* good. Medium rare, just the way he liked it.

They ate in a companionable silence during which Josh tried to think of a way to get her to leave even though he didn't want her to leave. And, as good as it was, he didn't want to be eating steak, either. He wanted to finish what they'd started two years ago. What they'd continued a week ago. What he'd been thinking about ever since.

"You know what I think?" she asked.

"Never." And that was the truth.

"You're afraid to become emotionally involved, so you're pushing me away."

"Not quite. I don't *want* to become emotionally involved. For long-term, women have a hard time with that."

"What's wrong with long-term?"

"What's wrong with short-term?" he countered.

"Not a thing." She popped a mushroom into her mouth and smiled.

He'd fallen into a trap. Josh felt the beginnings of

panic through the haze of desire. He didn't know how to handle panic because he never panicked. Panic was the result of fear and fear was an emotion. Emotions always caused trouble.

Sam was a walking emotion. Only right now, she was calmly—one might say unemotionally—eating.

Josh was not eating.

He fought to regain control. "You're not a short-term person."

"You're not an any-term person, and you know why?"

"Because I don't want to be."

"Because you don't want anyone to get to know you. Eat your steak."

Josh obediently ate some steak before he realized what he was doing. What she was doing. "People know me," he protested.

"Not the real you. You show them a charming facade and never stick around long enough for anyone to check behind the curtain. What's the matter? Afraid they won't like what they find?"

How could they? His own family didn't like him. Not his dad. His dad didn't really know him. But Josh's mother and sisters made no secret of the fact that they considered him fairly worthless. *You're just a good-looking charmer like your father. Sure, you get by now, but good looks don't last, and when they're gone, you'll have nothing.*

Nothing. He had nothing now.

Josh found it difficult to get a lungful of air. Sam...Sam wanted behind the curtain and he couldn't let her. "This is all about that night, isn't it?"

She got a guarded look on her face. "What night?"

"That's right, there's more than one. But I think this goes back to the first night. The one two years ago when you wanted to sleep with me and I didn't want to sleep with you."

Her face went white.

Josh felt ill, but made himself continue. "You've been trying to get back at me ever since. Well, you need to get over it. Guys get rejected all the time, but when a woman does, it's a Federal case."

"You were trying to seduce me—"

"Oh, please. There was no try. I could have had you and we both know it." *Slap my face. Get up and walk out now. Don't make me go on.*

"You only wanted the convention."

"I could have had the convention, too. You were just a little side bonus. A perk, if you will."

Sam looked as though she was the one who'd been slapped. Why didn't she leave?

"Why?" she whispered.

"Remember when I said everybody had a price? I was just trying to find yours."

Her face wore a devastated expression he hoped he'd never see again on her or any other woman. He could barely speak. "And as I recall, it was happy hour, so the price wasn't very..." He couldn't go on hurting her. He closed his eyes briefly, tightly, then opened them. "Do you hate me yet?"

11

SAM WOULD HAVE HATED Josh if he hadn't looked so agonized. She *should* have hated him. Wanted to hate him, but after the initial shock of what he was saying wore off, numbness set in, allowing her to understand what he was really doing.

And then he'd asked if she hated him and she'd just melted at his expression. He hadn't meant a word of it.

"Hate you? No." She shook her head, finding that, remarkably, she was as far from hating Josh as a person could be. Any desire for personal revenge evaporated.

He wanted her to like him and was afraid she wouldn't, therefore, he wouldn't give her the chance to really know him. It was so simple. Men were always trying to complicate things.

"I can't do this anymore," he whispered.

"Good, because it isn't very much fun."

"Not for me, either." He drew a deep breath. "Sam, I want you."

She smiled. "I know. I have evidence, remember?"

He gave her a half smile back. "About the stuff I said—"

"You were being noble. Trying to save me from myself."

"I'm fresh out of nobility."

"I'm glad."

They reached for each other at the same time.

The bar stools fell to the floor as Josh's mouth took hers in a kiss of breathless possession. And that was fine with Sam. More than fine, actually, especially since he also drew his arms tightly around her as if he never wanted to let go.

Sam didn't want him letting go. In the circle of his arms, she felt feminine and small. There weren't many men out there who could make Sam feel physically small and she reveled in the sensation.

But, courtesy of Josh, there were other sensations in which to revel, specifically, those caused by his mouth. Maybe it was because his mouth got so much exercise, but he had the nimblest pair of lips it had ever been her good fortune to encounter.

Josh may have been reluctant to acknowledge the long-standing attraction between them, but once he decided to act, he did so with gratifying enthusiasm.

"You feel so good in my arms," he murmured.

"I was thinking the same thing."

He looked down at her and brushed away a strand of her hair that was caught on her cheek. "You have the softest skin. I remember your skin. I dreamed about your skin—all the parts I touched and all the parts I didn't." He kissed her forehead and linked his arms loosely around her waist. "You're going to have to be the one who pulls away this time."

"I didn't want to pull away last time."

"I know." He rested his forehead against hers. "Neither did I. But being together wasn't right then."

"Is it right now?"

He sighed. "Probably not."

Sam dropped a light kiss on his lips. "Do you want it to be right?"

She heard the smile in his voice. "Yeah, I do."

When she didn't say anything, he prompted, "How about you? I'm serious—if you're going to leave, better make it quick."

"No, I can't leave. I..."

He leaned back so he could see her eyes. "What's the matter? Is this too quick, because—"

"No! No." She shook her head. "It's just that well, there was Kevin. He was a great guy and I think he loved me. I know I should have loved him. B-but..." And Sam, who was not a crier, felt her eyes sting with tears. She swallowed and sniffed. Hard. Still, she could only whisper the rest. "All you really did was kiss me and...and I felt more..."

Josh kissed her, a sweetly tender kiss that sent the tears leaking from the corners of her eyes. She *did* feel more for him—for a man she thought she hated, than for the man she thought she loved.

"Let's go to bed."

She nodded.

With a hand at the small of her back, Josh urged her toward the bedroom.

Even though the apartment was small, it seemed like there was a mile between the kitchen bar and the bedroom door.

Sam slowed down.

"Change your mind?" Josh asked at once.

"No!" She managed a watery smile. "Will you stop it? I'm not going to change my mind."

"But you're crying."

She wiped her eyes. "I'm not *crying*—well, I was, but only because I was thinking that if I'd made myself marry Kevin, then I wouldn't be here with you now because I wouldn't be in New York, I'd be a vet's wife in San Francisco and would be taken off the fast track and probably would have ended up with a desk job so I wouldn't have to travel as much and—"

"You talk a lot. I don't remember you talking so much."

"You've got something against talking? You were doing a lot of it earlier."

"That's because I was terrified of this."

"So you're the only one who's allowed to be terrified?"

"You're not terrified." He grinned at her. "I'm too good a kisser for that. You're quivering with anticipation."

"I could be quivering with terror."

"Oh, yeah?"

He swooped down and kissed her—hard, thoroughly and very satisfactorily, melting away the little bits of nervousness that had cropped up during the walk to his bedroom door. He kissed her, in fact, until her knees shook.

He chuckled. "Tell me what that is, huh?"

"Josh?"

"Mmm?" He bent to nuzzle the crook of her neck.

"I wasn't really terrified."

"I know, but I was. Am."

He ran his hands slowly up and down her arms and she realized Josh was a toucher, something that didn't surprise her. She remembered the look he'd given her earlier when she guessed that he craved affection.

Sam wasn't a toucher because it was safer for women in business not to be. She would have to remember to be physically demonstrative with Josh.

Shouldn't be difficult. "Why are you terrified?" She wrapped her arms around his waist and pressed her head against his chest.

She felt the tension ease out of him and smiled to herself.

"You're different. You—it'll mean more to wake up tomorrow with you beside me."

"What makes you think I'll stick around?"

"I could say that it's because I won't let you go, but the truth is, you won't want to leave."

Sam leaned back. "Just when I think you've turned into a decent human being..."

He laughed and tugged her toward the bedroom.

Sam tugged back. "Josh? Can you carry me?"

"You want to be carried?" He grinned. "A dyed-in-the-wool feminist like you?"

Sam felt herself blush. "Well, it's...it's kind of a fantasy. No man has ever been able to—"

Josh promptly swept her off her feet. Sam gasped. "You didn't hurt your back, did you?"

Josh gave her a look of pure disgust. "Now, is that what you say in your fantasy?"

"No, in my fantasy, I usually say, 'Oh, Brad.'"

"Brad?"

She gave an exaggerated sigh. "Or Russell."

"Russell?"

"If I'm in a toga mood. Well, it's *my* fantasy!"

"So who's making this fantasy happen, anyway? Let me hear a little oh, Joshing."

"Oh, Josh."

"Mmm. I'll have to see if I can't get a better 'oh, Josh' than that."

"You, sir, are welcome to try."

He—effortlessly, she was pleased to note—carried her into the bedroom. When he got to the bed he gave her an amused look and she knew, just *knew* that he was going to drop her on the bed. She flinched and tightened her hold around his neck.

But instead of dropping her, Josh cradled her to him until she could feel his heart pounding against hers. And he held her there, by the bed, long enough for her breathing to synchronize with his. He was cherishing the moment.

Cherishing her.

And that was all it took for Sam to realize that in spite of everything, in spite of fighting it for two years, in spite of all the one-upmanship between them, and sending her to Fiery Femmes—and then rescuing her—or maybe because of it, she'd fallen in love with Josh Crandall. Kicking and screaming all the way, but fallen nevertheless. Fallen hard.

How could she help herself? He'd been so transparently vulnerable, so desperate to be loved.

Even so, he was still a man and Sam knew that if she told him she loved him, he'd panic.

Sam was still a little shaky on the concept, herself.

THERE WAS SO MUCH HE wanted to say to her yet couldn't find the words. Finally, he set her on the bed and sat next to her. "Thanks for not leaving." It wasn't the most romantic thing to say, but this apartment wasn't the most romantic setting, except for the fact that Sam was here.

She slipped off her shoes and leaned back. "Oh, I expect you'll make it worth my while."

"You got that right." It would all have to be up to him, though. This wasn't even a king-size bed. No flowers. No satin sheets. No room service. No smoke and mirrors.

He flipped on the bedside lamp and they both grimaced in the bright light.

"I can fix that." With her eyes on his, Sam unbuttoned her pink blouse and draped it over the lamp.

Instantly, the room light softened and her eyes went dark and mysterious.

Sam was here. Incredibly, she was here with him. Something squeezed his heart.

"You're beautiful," he whispered. She was so beautiful, it almost hurt to look at her. But, he'd force himself.

She made a face and gestured to her chest. "I'm not wearing my date underwear. I do have some, but—"

"But it's not going to stay on long enough to matter, anyway."

"It's not?"

Josh stood, started unbuttoning his shirt and quickly pulled it off. "Not."

Sam stared at him, her lips parted.

Pleased at her expression, he managed to refrain from flexing his muscles. Inhaling to pull in his gut didn't count.

Licking her lips, she said, "If I've failed to mention it before, uh, hubba hubba."

"Hotel gyms. You like?" Propping his arms on either side of her, he bent down and kissed her.

"I like." Sam took the opportunity to run her hands over his shoulders and back. "I like a lot."

He closed his eyes, enjoying her touch, then reluctantly stood again before he started to purr.

"Uh, one more thing—"

"There's a box in the drawer."

Sam gingerly tugged on the rickety nightstand drawer and looked inside. "What, you buy in bulk?"

He smiled. "You'll be glad later."

She smiled back.

Man, he lo—wanted this woman. Unbuckling his belt, he asked, "Do you have any other fantasies I should know about?"

"No, you're doing just fine." She motioned with her hand. "Carry on."

"*I've* got a fantasy. I'd like to undress in front of a naked woman."

"That can be arranged. Does she just appear naked, or are you actively involved with getting her to her naked state?"

"I can't be actively involved. I'm too busy getting naked, myself."

"Ah." Sam stood, unfastened her skirt, then stopped. "Josh, do you like my skirt?"

Josh kicked off his shoes and pulled off his pants. Usually at this point in the proceedings, his opinion on clothing was moot. "Do you want me to like your skirt?" It was a black skirt, not particularly tight or short. He didn't see anything special about it.

"I just thought..."

Josh gave the skirt a tug until it pooled at her feet. "I like the way it comes off."

He started to do the same with his boxers, but Sam stopped him.

"I thought you said your fantasy was to undress in front of a naked woman."

"It was." Josh pulled off his boxers. "But you've got a parochial schoolgirl thing going with that underwear. I like it. It's kind of kinky."

Sam gasped. "That's—that's..." She immediately shed her underwear.

"Ah. A naked woman." Josh reached for her. "I'm good, aren't I?"

"That remains to be seen."

As he held her lush body next to his, Josh vowed that this would be for Sam. All for her. He would give her more pleasure than she could handle because he had a lot to make up to her.

But Sam had other ideas. She met him kiss for kiss and touch for touch. Her mouth explored him as his explored her. When he settled her into the mattress with hot, deep kisses, he felt her tremble. Yet he trembled, too.

He stroked her, remembering the feel of her body, learning new curves and hollows. She did the same, following the movements of her hands with her eyes, concentrating, giving the faintest of smiles when he caught his breath.

It wasn't enough. He had to be closer. As he nudged

her thighs apart, Sam wrapped her legs around him and Josh felt blissed out with the pleasure of it. But then she squirmed out from under him and pushed him on his back, lacing her fingers with his and lying on top of him. Her hair curtained their faces as she kissed him as deeply as he'd kissed her.

Somewhere in the part of his brain still capable of rational thought, Josh remembered that he was supposed to be making love to her, not the other way around. *He* wanted to hear her moan as he brought her to the brink.

But he was the one who was at the brink.

He dragged his mouth away and struggled to sit up. "Sam..." It was a groan. "I want—"

"Shh." She put a finger against his lips. "Let me."

And so help him, he did. He surrendered to Sam.

Wearing a look of fierce sensuality, Sam lowered herself onto him, enveloping him in moist heat. He caught his breath as the sensation threatened to overwhelm him.

When he opened his eyes, he saw that she was watching him, satisfied with his reaction. *She* was taking *him*. And he didn't care.

Josh grabbed her flanks as she shifted, seeking the rhythm she needed. Moving his hands down to her hips, he felt her muscles bunch as she raised and lowered herself. The sensation was incredibly erotic.

She moved faster and faster, her lower lip caught between her teeth, her eyes squeezed shut in concentration.

Josh bit his tongue, determined to outlast her.

It was a losing battle.

Yielding to the inevitable, Josh tightened his hold on her hips and thrust upward.

Sam gasped. "Oh, Josh!" Her eyes opened in surprise.

Josh felt her tense, then watched as her forehead smoothed and a smile of supreme satisfaction crossed her face. With a final thrust, he lost himself within her.

He'd never lost himself with any woman before, never completely surrendered to the moment. He'd always held something of himself back, a lot of himself, he realized as he gathered her boneless body to him.

But Sam had demanded all of him. Not just physical intimacy, but emotional intimacy as well. The whole package.

It was so great. Scary, but great.

They lay, just breathing. And for Josh, the scary faded leaving just the great part.

"Mmm." Sam stretched. "Well?"

Yes, well. "Next time, I get to be on top," he murmured.

Sam raised herself on an elbow. "When does next time start?"

Josh eased her onto her back and captured her arms at the wrists. Slowly, he began kissing his way down her body. "Next time has already begun."

PLEASED WITH HERSELF, Sam, exhausted, fully sated, and very, very relaxed, turned onto her side. Josh immediately fit his body around hers and she sighed happily.

"I adore you," he whispered, his breath warming her cheek.

Adoration wasn't the same as love, but Sam could handle being adored for now.

SAM AWOKE AND LISTENED to Josh's even breathing, feeling very content. What would it be like to awaken this way every morning? In her heart, she knew she wanted to.

Yeah, she loved him, the big lug. He probably loved her, too, but he wasn't going to admit it anytime soon. She understood perfectly. She'd been in love with him for ages and hadn't wanted to admit it even to herself.

So now what?

The phone jangled in the silence, startling her.

"Go 'way," Josh mumbled.

"Okay."

"Not you. The world. Unless you're going away to fix breakfast."

"We ate steak at midnight. How can you be hungry?"

"Hmm." He smiled.

"I can't stand it. Answer the phone!"

Josh grimaced and picked up the phone.

Sam slid out of bed and looked around for something to put on. There was the ever popular putting on the man's shirt, but, realistically, she had to get back to her place and change for work. Not that she wanted to.

"Yes?" The tone of Josh's voice changed. He'd answered the phone in a gruff what-are-you-doing-calling-so-early voice. He now sounded completely alert.

Okay. Sam put back on her comfortable schoolgirl underwear—for the last time—and retrieved her blouse from the lamp shade. Grabbing the rest of her clothes, she crept from the room to give Josh some privacy.

She was completely dressed and hacking at one of Josh's bagels when he emerged from the bedroom.

He draped his arms around her from the back and nuzzled her neck. "Don't go."

"I've got to."

"You could be late..." He tried tugging her back to the bedroom.

Sam had a sudden vision of this morning being multiplied by years of mornings in which she was torn between Josh and her work.

But that wasn't fair. Still, everything her mother had drilled into her about charting her own course and not tying herself to a man reverberated through her mind.

And she remembered Chris, her sister, being so relieved that Sam had a promotion in the works. Chris had looked so haggard trying to deal with work, pregnancy, and mother a toddler.

She was getting way, way ahead of herself. "Josh..."

"Yeah, you're right." He sat on a bar stool and watched her prepare the bagels. "That was Meckler on the phone. The Family Values Assembly does want to cancel. We get to counter."

Sam would have expected it. "I don't have a problem with that. It's business."

A couple of beats went by. "My severance agreement says that I'm to be available to handle any problems with my major accounts, so...I'm the one who'll be countering."

Sam turned around and faced him. "And so what, you expect me to be mad?"

Josh was staring down at his hands. "It'll be awkward."

"It doesn't have to be awkward." In fact, Sam realized how much she wanted—needed—to go head-to-head one more time with Josh.

He looked up. "They want us there at the same time."

"When?"

"Today. This morning, if we can, but more likely right after lunch."

Sam gasped. "And you're just now telling me?"

"I just found out."

"But you found out and you wanted to...to..." She stared at him. "Say we'd gone back to bed. Would you have let me leave without telling me? Knowing that I'd not get the message until later? Maybe too late?"

"No, Sam. I'm not so threatened by your phenomenal salesmanship that I'd try to make you miss the meeting." His voice softened. "I just wanted to make love with you again and I hoped you'd want to make love with me again, too."

"Because you think this meeting will change things between us." She was afraid it might have already changed things between them.

"Maybe," he said. "What if I asked you not to go?"

"What if I asked *you* not to go?"

"I'm contractually obligated to go. I'd get sued."

"Well, I'm...morally obligated to go. Do not try to turn this into some kind of relationship test." Sam abandoned the bagel. Let him get his own breakfast.

"Let's neither one of us go to the meeting."

He was serious. He was actually serious.

Shaking her head, Sam tucked in her blouse and put on her jacket. "You know how important this is to me. You know how much I want the promotion with Carrington."

He leaned back, his eyes dark. "I know your mother wants it. She wants it bad—how many sisters do you have? And she's disappointed in all of you? She wants you to become a corporate bigwig to justify her choices in life."

Sam slung her purse over her shoulder. "So you're back to saying bad things so I'll leave. Fine."

"Wrong. I want you to go after what you want because it *is* what you want, not because it's what your mother wants for you."

"How fortunate that we both want the same thing." She headed for the door.

"So where do I fit in?"

The question stopped her. Men. Why did everything always have to be about them? "Josh...all that's happening here is that I'm leaving to get ready for the meeting. I'll see you there." She smiled, hoping to coax one out of him. "And you better give this your best shot because I'll be insulted if you don't."

"WELL, WELL, WELL." A.J. looked up from her coffee when Sam came racing in. "Do I take it the skirt worked its magic?"

"Maybe." Sam looked down. The skirt. "I'd better wear it today even though people are going to think I don't have anything else."

"But we don't know if that's the skirt." Claire appeared at the door of her office bedroom and exchanged a look with A.J.

"I changed into a skirt on my bed." Sam had a bad feeling about this.

"Yeah, well, there were two black skirts in my closet yesterday morning—yours and my copy. Did you take the right one?"

Sam hadn't seen A.J.'s knockoff. *Had* she worn the right one? "Let's compare."

Her two roommates got their respective black skirts and brought them next to the living room window.

"They look just alike," A.J. said. "Which one is it, Sam?"

Sam looked down at the one she wore, then at the others. Nothing. No gleam. No glimmer. "I don't know. I can't tell. But I've got a meeting in a couple of hours, so we need to figure it out by then."

ONLY THEY HADN'T BEEN able to figure it out. Sam was wearing a black skirt all right, but she absolutely couldn't tell if it was The Skirt.

She and Josh sat at a conference table—both in the middle—with the Family Values Assembly board. Since she was sitting, the skirt wasn't visible, so Sam supposed it didn't matter.

She was going to have to win the convention on her own.

"Thank you both for appearing before us on such short notice," Mr. Carelle, the chairman, said.

"I appreciate that everyone's time is at a premium,"

Josh interrupted, to Sam's surprise. She was even more surprised at what he said next.

"I've reviewed Ms. Baldwin's proposal and it's absolutely the one you should go with. We can't touch it."

"I appreciate your honesty, Mr. Crand—"

"Wait a minute!" What was Josh doing? Torpedoing his own bid, that's what. Sam wasn't going to win like that. She'd *told* him she'd wanted him to try his best because if she was going to win she wanted to win by being the best. And she had to win this one time if they ever had a chance to be together.

She spoke, "You had a prior agreement and long-standing relationship with Meckler. Their proposal could be improved by adding a couple of entertainments for middle-grade children and the wives. That wouldn't be difficult."

Josh didn't even look at her. "However, the Carrington Washington, D. C., is the better location."

"For people on the east coast, sure, but it will increase costs for those coming in from the west. The Meckler in Chicago is more centrally located."

Naturally Josh countered with some other nonsense, so Sam did as well. The eyes of the Family Values Board ping-ponged between the two of them. Finally, they called a recess to discuss the situation.

They asked Josh and Sam to leave.

Sam could barely contain herself until they were in the hallway outside the conference room. "What do you think you're doing?" she demanded.

"Helping you get your promotion. What do you think *you're* doing?"

"I didn't want it that way. I want them to decide that my proposal is the best."

"It is the best. That's what I told them."

"But—"

"Sam." Josh slumped onto the arm of the sofa in one of the little oasis seating areas dotting the long hallway. "This is all about competing. We're always competing. In everything. Dinner last night. Making love last night. We just competed in *not* competing."

"That's not..." But it was.

"I need a break," he said.

"We spend one night together and you're already talking about a break?"

"I mean from the competing. I do it every day, I don't want to do it in my home life, too. And I don't want to have to compete with your job for your attention. I want you all to myself. There it is."

"You're not being fair." Sam paced in front of him.

"I'm being honest. Isn't that fair?"

"You want a Fiery Femme wife! You want somebody to cater to you."

"Maybe." Josh stood and reached for her, holding her tightly until the stiffness went out of her arms and she linked them around him. "But most of all, I want to be enough for somebody." He released her. "And you need more. And that's okay, Sam." His smile was a ghost of his Josh smile. "Have a good life."

And he turned and walked out of hers.

HAVE A GOOD LIFE? *Have a good life?* Well, that had to be the shortest, deepest, most wrenchingly intense relationship in the history of relationships. Emphasis on the shortest. Emphasis on intense. Oh, heck. Emphasis on wrenching, too.

When she got back to her office, she learned that Family Values had gone with Carrington. Big surprise.

Sam got her promotion, becoming the first woman manager in Carrington's history. Also big surprise, since Leonard Sheffield had bombed with some program and Harvey Wannerstein had gone AWOL.

She could just strangle Josh. Couldn't he trust her to do anything on her own?

At least Sam could call her mother. Maybe then she'd feel more like celebrating.

When she got back to her apartment that evening, Sam closed the door to her bedroom and called her mother, who was euphoric. She babbled about what a victory it was and the long road it had been and so on and on and on. The whole time, Josh's words echoed in her mind. *Your mother wants you to succeed to justify her own choices.* Or something stupid like that.

At last, Sam's mother wound down. "Sam, aren't you happy?"

Was she happy? "No."

There was a shocked silence. "Why not?" came the inevitable question.

"Because I've fallen in love and I can't have both Josh and my job. And I hate that."

"Josh? Is this the Josh—"

"Yes." Sam didn't want to talk about Josh with her mother.

Her mother was silent. "Oh, Sam." She sighed. "I don't want you to be unhappy, truly I don't. Chris has given me what for because I made her feel guilty about her decision to stay home and raise her kids. I never meant to. I just wanted to make sure you girls didn't make the same mistakes I saw so many women make. They'd give up everything for their men and were left with nothing for themselves."

"Is that what we are to you? Nothing?"

"No! I just wanted to encourage you to reach as high as you could. When I worked at the employment agency, I saw women who'd stopped their schooling, or hadn't worked their entire married lives. Their marriages failed and they had no resources. No training. No self-confidence. My girls weren't going to make those mistakes."

Sam felt better after talking with her mother, then she got angry. Marriage and family or a spectacular career. Why was it always the woman who had to choose?

She decided to ask Josh, Mr. I-should-be-enough-for-any-woman. Thinking over last night, Sam could see where he got that idea—there might be the slightest justification—but still.

Yes, she'd go ask Josh, but first, she was going to change into the skirt. If it was supposed to attract her one, true love, then she wanted it attracting Josh.

She found her roommates watching one of Tavish's videos. "Hey, do we know which skirt is which, yet?"

Glumly, they shook their heads.

Great. She was going to have to do this on her own, too.

HE SHOULD HAVE KNOWN that he couldn't keep Sam. Being with her was both exhilarating and exhausting, and Josh was tired. It wasn't so much that he expected the woman in his life to wait on him like a slave, but he did want her there for him. And he wanted to be there for her, too.

After leaving Sam with the FVA board, Josh went shopping, of all things. He bought a bed comforter. In blue. He liked blue. And he bought the fancy pillows that went with it. And sheets. And then he bought towels. And a candle that smelled flowery like the lotion Sam wore.

He carted that all up to his apartment, then went back and bought a framed poster that he liked. And a lamp. And something called a slipcover that he could tie over the ugly sofa.

He now owned more stuff than he'd ever owned in his life. The thing was, he wanted a home. And he hadn't realized it until Sam. Maybe if he had the home, it wouldn't hurt so much that he didn't have Sam.

SAM WAS NERVOUS AS SHE knocked on Josh's apartment door. She hadn't even called to tell him she was coming over. They'd said he'd gone home when she'd checked at the office, but that didn't mean he *was* at home. He was probably out getting dinner, or something.

The door opened and he stood there. His face lit up, then, then he slapped on the old affable Josh mask.

Sam hated the Josh mask.

"I hear congratulations are in order."

"What, did you bug Hennesey's office, or something?" Sam took it upon herself to walk in, since he didn't invite her.

The first thing she noticed was that he was tying a

taupe-colored damask slipcover over the sofa. Or attempting to.

"What's all this?"

"Doing a little redecorating. I've had a couple of calls for seminars, so it looks like I'll be sticking around New York for a while."

Sam's heart began to pound even more than it already was. Okay. It was time to go for it. She was going to win something over him and this was the only thing worth winning. She inhaled and resolutely faced him. "Josh..."

The Josh mask had disappeared. "I love you, Sam. I'm sorry I'm not enough for you."

"You're going to make me cry, you goof!" She sniffed. This wasn't the argument she'd prepared. "You're plenty for me. But I can handle you and a job, too. Why do I have to make a choice? Tell me why. Why does it always have to be the woman?"

"It doesn't." His calm voice contrasted with Sam's. "Do you want me to give up my job?"

"Do you want to give up your job?"

"No."

"Why? Aren't I enough for you?"

He leaned back against the half-covered sofa. "I'm beginning to think you're *too* much for me."

"It's the competing thing, isn't it? Well, I've thought about what you said and I don't think I have a solution, except that I want to try to work it out."

When Josh said nothing, Sam babbled on. How could he just give up before they had very much to give up? She didn't want to lose him.

Face set, Josh walked toward her.

"We could go to counseling," Sam said desperately, "or maybe since you'll be giving seminars and I'll be managing, and we won't be competing professionally anymore—"

"You *do* talk a lot and when you're talking, I can't kiss you."

Sam shut up.

Josh held her face in his hands and kissed all the words out of her. "You just won't go away, will you?"

She shook her head.

"Did you hear me tell you I loved you?"

"Yes, but it kind of got lost. I knew it, anyway."

"Oh, you did." He smiled at her in a way she'd never seen before. Tender and rueful at the same time.

Sam nodded. "I'm glad you told me, so that I know you realize it and I can tell you I love you without scaring you off."

He laughed softly. "You still talk too much."

"You know, we can work this out, if you want to," she said. "Just like a bid package." She sensed victory. He'd told her he loved her—that was a victory, wasn't it?

"Not *exactly* like a bid package. More like a proposal. I want you in my life, Sam, and I want to be in yours."

Now that was a victory. Definitely one for the win column—the only win she'd ever need. She felt the smile stretch across her face. *Now* she was happy. "Mmm. I like proposals much better than bids. You know why?"

Smiling, he shook his head.

"Because we can seal them with a kiss."

Josh took hold of her hands and pulled her toward the bedroom. "I think we can seal our proposal with something a lot better than that."

And he even let her be on top.

Epilogue

"HEY, FRANCO, HOW'S IT going?"

"Josh, my man, what do you know?" Franco had already whipped out his cell phone.

Sam just smiled. Josh had become Franco's main source of gossip. She already knew what Josh was going to tell him, but Josh got such a kick out of Franco's reaction, that he wanted to relay the news in person.

"Joey Fuentes and Marco 'The Terminator' Thompson?"

"Yes, yes."

"Phht. Kaput." Josh gestured with his hands. "A room service breakfast for two was served to Marco and..."

"Yes?" Franco nearly stood on his toes with excitement.

"Tiffany Royale."

"No!" Franco gasped and clutched his chest. "That might be a stage name?"

Josh and Sam walked toward the elevator. "Room service says there was a stage body to go with it."

"Oh. My. Gawwwwd." Franco misdialed twice before the elevator arrived.

"I like Franco," Josh said after they got into the elevator. "Little things thrill him."

Sam laced her fingers through his. "Yeah. I'm going to miss him when I move out. I can't believe it's nearly the end of the summer."

Josh grinned. "You've all but moved out anyway, so it's about time I got to meet your roommates."

"Well, you know, everybody's schedule is rough these days."

"And you wanted me all to yourself."

"And I wanted you all to myself."

But tonight was boyfriend night when everybody was going to meet everybody else. Josh was a hit with A.J. and Claire, as Sam had known he would be.

But before the other boyfriends arrived, Sam had some unfinished business with her roommates. Sending Josh to the kitchen to open a bottle of wine, she pulled them aside.

"Okay. The skirt."

"I knew you were going to bring that up," moaned Claire.

"So we still can't tell them apart?" A.J. looked disgusted.

"What are we going to do?" Claire asked. "We've got to figure out some way to tell which skirt is which, but how?"

Sam couldn't get too worked up. After all, it was supposed to attract her one true love and meeting Josh's gaze as he crossed the room toward her with the wine and glasses, she knew that the skirt had worked for her.

*   *   *   *   *

The skirt strikes again! But who is its next target—
Claire or A.J.? Find out next month in
        SHEERLY IRRESISTIBLE
        by Kristin Gabriel.

LIVE THE EMOTION

Modern Romance™
...seduction and
passion guaranteed

Tender Romance™
...love affairs that
last a lifetime

Medical Romance™
...medical drama
on the pulse

Historical Romance™
...rich, vivid and
passionate

Sensual Romance™
...sassy, sexy and
seductive

Blaze Romance™
...the temperature's
rising

27 new titles every month.

Live the emotion

MILLS & BOON®

MB3

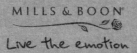

Live the emotion

... and get carried away with these three red-hot reads!

Miranda Lee
Caroline Anderson
Julia Byrne

MILLS & BOON

Available from 20th June 2003

Available at most branches of WH Smith,
Tesco, Martins, Borders, Eason, Sainsbury's
and all good paperback bookshops.

0703/024/MB77

Don't miss *Book Eleven* of this BRAND-NEW 12 book collection 'Bachelor Auction'.

Who says money can't buy love?

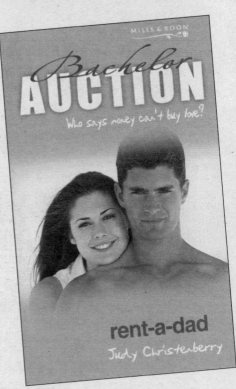

On sale 4th July

FREE

2 BOOKS
AND A SURPRISE GIFT!

We would like to take this opportunity to thank you for reading this Mills & Boon® book by offering you the chance to take TWO more specially selected titles from the Sensual Romance™ series absolutely FREE! We're also making this offer to introduce you to the benefits of the Reader Service™—

- ★ FREE home delivery
- ★ FREE monthly Newsletter
- ★ FREE gifts and competitions
- ★ Exclusive Reader Service discount
- ★ Books available before they're in the shops

Accepting these FREE books and gift places you under no obligation to buy; you may cancel at any time, even after receiving your free shipment. Simply complete your details below and return the entire page to the address below. *You don't even need a stamp!*

YES! Please send me 2 free Sensual Romance™ books and a surprise gift. I understand that unless you hear from me, I will receive 4 superb new titles every month for just £2.60 each, postage and packing free. I am under no obligation to purchase any books and may cancel my subscription at any time. The free books and gift will be mine to keep in any case.

T3ZEC

Ms/Mrs/Miss/Mr ....Initials ....
BLOCK CAPITALS PLEASE

Surname ....

Address ....

....

....Postcode ....

Send this whole page to:
UK: FREEPOST CN81, Croydon, CR9 3WZ
EIRE: PO Box 4546, Kilcock, County Kildare (stamp required)

Offer valid in UK and Eire only and not available to current Reader Service subscribers to this series. We reserve the right to refuse an application and applicants must be aged 18 years or over. Only one application per household. Terms and prices subject to change without notice. Offer expires 30th September 2003. As a result of this application, you may receive offers from Harlequin Mills & Boon and other carefully selected companies. If you would prefer not to share in this opportunity please write to The Data Manager at the address above.

Mills & Boon® is a registered trademark owned by Harlequin Mills & Boon Limited.
Sensual Romance™ is a registered trademark used under licence.